BECOMING

BECOMING

Charlotte Vale Allen

This title first published in Great Britain 1994 by
SEVERN HOUSE PUBLISHERS LTD of
9–15 High Street, Sutton, Surrey SM1 1DF.
First published in hardcover format in the USA 1994 by
SEVERN HOUSE PUBLISHERS INC., of
425 Park Avenue, New York, NY 10022.

British Library Cataloguing in Publication Data
Allen, Charlotte Vale
  Becoming. – New ed
  I. Title
  813.54 [F]

  ISBN 0-7278-4659-0

Typeset by Hewer Text Composition Services, Edinburgh.
Printed and bound in Great Britain by
Hartnolls Ltd, Bodmin, Cornwall.

BECOMING

ONE

It happened while she was stirring the lemon juice into the pan, hurrying so that the veal wouldn't go cold. Suddenly, without warning, she'd arrived at the end.

"I'm leaving," she said aloud. Amazed at herself. She went right on pouring the lemon-butter sauce over the veal—her bastardized version of veal piccata—able, for a moment, to enjoy the aroma of the food.

"Leaving what?" Frank said.

She looked up at him then, wondering why she'd chosen this particular moment. Yet she felt her face forming itself into an unfamiliar expression. Her face was deadly serious, angry, alert and ready for battle. He smiled because it had to be some kind of joke.

"What are you saying?" he asked, thinking this was a lousy time for a conversation. The food would go cold.

"You know," she said evenly, toying with the

9

wooden spoon she'd been using to stir the sauce, "that's one of the reasons I'm going."

"What? What reason? What?"

"You don't listen. Do you know that? You never listen. And you don't have anything to say either. I'm leaving."

"You're leaving," he repeated stupidly.

Her appetite had vanished. The smell of the veal suddenly made her feel faintly nauseated. That and the words, thoughts fighting their way into her brain like frenzied women battling their way toward a bargain.

"That's right. I'm going to leave." Her throat was throbbing. A small animal racing back and forth in the cage of her neck. "I'm sick of this."

"You're sick of this." He kept waiting for the punchline. For the joke. Something. This wasn't real, wasn't actually happening. Then there was a kind of click in his brain and his responses seemed to snap into action. "You're sick of this," he said again. "*I'm* sick of this."

He was going to turn everything around, going to claim the initiative as his own. She could see it and stood, stunned, watching the anger transform his features. He turned and marched out of the kitchen.

"Sick of this, eh?" he said. "You're sick of this. *I'm* the one. Me."

Dazed, she followed him, wiping her sweating palms down the front of her apron. They made a small parade that came to a halt in the bedroom where he flung open the closet door, grabbed two suitcases and tossed them—the lids opening with the force of the gesture—onto the bed. Then he started opening the dresser drawers, lifting out armloads of shirts, underwear, socks. And she stood beside the bed watching the shirts she'd ironed and the underwear she'd laundered and the socks she'd carefully folded one inside the other and rolled into neat little balls all get dropped into one of the suitcases. Dazed. The bastard had reversed their roles, making himself the decision-maker; robbing her of her moment even in this.

"I'm the one who's leaving," she said, amazed as always at how easily he was able to achieve an upper hand.

"Nobody walks out on me," he said, on the go, moving back and forth, sucking things out of the drawers with his arms like a human vacuum cleaner. "I'm getting the hell out of here."

"Frank, this is stupid," she began, then stopped.

"Right!" He snapped the locks on the first suitcase. "Goddamned stupid. To put up with . . . you're no prize, Sid. You know that? You're fat. You're lazy as hell. Who needs this? I don't need this."

How did this get turned around? she wondered, automatically smoothing the bedspread, struggling to come to terms with the unexpected flood of outrage sweeping over her.

"Where do you think you're going to go?" she asked, chewing on her lower lip, hating the way he was forcing her into the defensive.

"Somewhere," he said, haphazardly folding a suit

11

into the second bag, then going back to the closet to lift down another suit—hanger and all—and push it into the suitcase on top of the first one. "Nobody's pushing me out of my own house!"

"Nobody said anything about pushing," she said. "I said I was going to leave and somehow you're the one who's leaving. You always do this," she said, somewhat breathlessly. "I . . . eight years. It's long enough. We sit in the living room every night with the set on while I read the local newspaper and you read your evening newspaper and Walter Cronkite . . . It's as if we're *old*. I'm too young . . . I'm stagnating out here."

"And what'm I supposed to do?" he asked hotly, glaring at her.

Her throat felt sticky, reluctant to let words pass through. She half wished this hadn't ever started.

"You . . . there's no reason for that," she indicated the bags. "I thought I'd just . . ." Again she stopped. She had no idea of what she'd thought she'd do. She hadn't thought.

"There's all kinds of reasons," he said. "I guess you'll have to put the house up for sale. I need the money."

"What do you mean you need the money?" She had the feeling now that they were talking about entirely different things.

"You started this," he said threateningly. "It would've been fine. Just remember you were the one who started."

"What?" She stared at him, bewildered.

"I would've given you more time," he said. "But

you forced this whole thing. I'm going to need the money."

"Why?"

"Because," he said defiantly, "I'm going to marry somebody else. And we're going to need the money."

She sat down on the side of the bed thinking, He's lying. Retaliating. Drumming up the most hurtful things he can think of to say because I said I wanted to leave. And I can't be the one to make decisions —of any kind. So now, now he's going to punish me.

"You can just climb up off your duff and do something. Eight years you've been feeding off me like some kind of goddamned parasite. It's about time you did something. You're not crippled. Go out and get a job."

With that, he hefted the bags off the bed, marched out of the bedroom and through the living room to the front door where he parked the bags. Reaching into his pocket, he extracted his wallet and pulled out several bills.

"Here's a hundred," he said, waving the money at her. "Take it! I'll give you another one in a couple of weeks. After that, we'll let our lawyers decide how much you're going to get. But it won't be much, Sid. So I'm telling you, you'd better move your ass. I don't know what the hell you'll do," he said, a gleam of malicious satisfaction in his eyes. He'd won, he believed. Moved himself right into the driver's seat. "I mean, about the only thing you're any good at is cooking. It's not much to get a job on."

He opened the door, picked up the bags and

carried them down to the front walk to where the car was parked. Like some kind of windup toy —so furious she couldn't think of one coherent thing to say—she chased along after him, watching as he opened the trunk, lifted the bags inside, closed the trunk, then dusted off his hands and turned to face her.

"Listen," she said, trying to get him to stop moving. "Listen!"

He paused dramatically, faking a smile, his hand on the car. Waiting. Pretending he was prepared to listen.

"You always do this," she gasped out the words. "Always. This time . . . I made the decision. But you always have trump cards you've been saving. Always." She looked confused, felt horribly frustrated at not being able to put the proper words to her anger. She squinted into the early evening summer sunshine, willing the words to come to her; willing her mouth to open and let fly all the stingingly articulate expletives, curses. They wouldn't come. "Where are you going?" she asked finally, momentarily defeated.

"Away from here," he said summarily. "Who the hell d'you think you are anyway telling me you're leaving? I'm the one doing the leaving."

He got in the car, started the engine and drove away.

She stood there a long time, long after the car had vanished from sight. Just like that. In about fifteen minutes he'd robbed her of everything. Again. Taken the decision from her, usurped her right to make decisions or take stances. Like the supporting act determined to outshine the star, he'd seen her intention, noted her direction and leaped in to force her off the road and race on past her.

She turned and walked back up to the house, to sit down in the rocker in the living room, moving back and forth, trying to make sense of him, of what he'd done.

Tears welled up in her eyes, spilled over and snaked down her cheeks. Eight years. Being what you wanted me to be, Frank. When I was twenty, you said you wanted me because I was exactly the kind of girl you'd always hoped to find. Someone who wanted a home, a husband; someone who loved to cook, and preferred a quiet life. I never had any other ambition then. Just you. But what you wanted was someone you could best, someone you could control. I'm fat and lazy. Bastard. No chance even to state my case. Taking everything, even my right to say I've had enough. Creating another woman, creating a need for money. Why didn't I create another man? No chance. There was no chance. You rush away and I'm still here where I don't want to be.

All at once, she couldn't bear sitting there, swaying back and forth in the rocker. She got up and went into the bedroom to take off all her clothes and look at herself in the mirror. To look at herself and feel the anger throbbing in her temples, beating at the sides of her skull, seeing the pads of flesh on her hips and the roll of fat around her middle. And her breasts huge. How did I let this happen? she wondered, moving closer to the mirror to get a better view. A closeup of bulging thighs and a pendulous rear end. And her face. Pudgy. And I refused to let myself notice. You. You ate everything I cooked, making such a fuss, smacking your lips, saying, "Terrific. Really terrific, Sid." A ploy. Keep her busy at the stove and she won't have time for any thinking. But I sneaked a little time to myself and the decision got made and you couldn't allow that. Look! A forty-five-year-old body and I'm only twenty-nine. Why did I let this happen?

She pulled on her robe and wandered out to the kitchen to dump the dinner into the garbage, then replaced the dishes on the shelves and started cleaning the skillet. When suddenly anger was a tidal wave that crashed down on her and, vibrating with fury, she pulled the skillet out of the soapy water and hurled it with all her might through the kitchen window, hearing the glass shatter and the thud of the pan landing on the grass outside. She punched out the bits of glass still clinging to the frame until none remained. All the edges clean, glass-free. Air flowing serenely through the now permanently open window.

She backed away, turned out the kitchen light and went to stand in the middle of the living room, distantly aware of pain in her hands as she turned to look at this living room she was going to leave, at this house she had to escape. The pain finally caught her attention and she looked down at her tightly clenched hands to see them smeared with blood. Blood dripping on the carpet. Dry-eyed, rage a hollow yet substantial blockage in her chest, she walked through to the bathroom to hold both her hands under the cold water faucet. And finally, with frozen, numbed hands, she lay down on top of the bed in her robe, staring at the ceiling for what seemed like hours until suddenly it was morning and she'd slept. The night was over. The first night she'd slept alone in more than eight years. And that was some sort of minor victory.

With morning, she was better able to examine Frank's actions without the off-balance perspective of the night before. Her determination returned. Frank's departure had been only for effect, the sort of thing he felt obliged to do in order to keep her in her place. Give her a day or two and she'd fall back into line. But not this time. Coupled with something that felt like a very real injury somewhere on her person was an anger that gathered force with each passing moment. So that when he called as usual mid-morning, magnanimously prepared to accept her apology and return home, she greeted him in a barely controlled voice saying, "I'm not changing my mind. You can *have* this house. Obviously, you're going to be needing it if you're going to start another marriage with someone else. I'll be leaving as soon as I can pack. I'll let you know where to reach me."

Unable to trust herself to conversation beyond this point, she hung up and hurried to the bathroom to shower, make up and ready herself to follow

17

through on this decision. I've decided and I won't allow you to maneuver me into a corner.

Her breathing was fast and shallow, her heartbeat rapid as she hurried through showering and making up, dressing in the dreadful navy dress that had been Frank's favorite, rushing out of the house to the car she had bought before her marriage. She drove straight to the bank.

With a thumping feeling of success pounding guiltily in her ribcage, she withdrew the entire balance of seven thousand, eight hundred and twelve dollars and sixteen cents from the savings account. It's mine, she told herself, waiting while the teller prepared a cashier's check. It's my money. I worked for it. You get the house. I'll take the money. It's fair. My labor is worth something.

She fled back to the car considering the question of fairness. Turning everything around so he could be the one to leave. I'm taking the money. That's fair. She slid into the driver's seat, and all at once her momentum was gone. What do I do now? All this money. I'm leaving. Going somewhere. The air left her lungs in one long, slow exhalation. What do I do next?

Think! she told herself, gazing blankly through the windshield. This is what you wanted. Think carefully! Try to form a plan. Be realistic. Seven, almost eight thousand dollars. It won't last all that long. It's expensive to live. I have to live somewhere. She pictured herself installed someplace snug where she could sit very quietly and think, determine priorities. Yes. I must have somewhere to think. That comes first. Most important.

She started the car and drove a few blocks to the main street, parking the car in the lot behind the stores. She picked up a newspaper at the corner store, then continued on to the coffee shop where she settled herself at the counter. The look and smell of the breakfasts others were eating was sickening. Feeling highly visible, as though everyone must know she was running away from home, she ordered coffee. Opened the paper to "Apartments to Rent Unfurnished" and with a marker in hand, began carefully scanning the ads. First things first. Vital to find a place. Once I find a place, then I'll be able to decide on the next step.

With four specific ads circled, she got five dimes from the bleary-eyed waitress, went to the pay phone beside the front door and started calling. One was already taken. Three were still available and she made appointments to view them. Excitement back again, knocking in her chest, she felt decidedly proud and returned to the counter to have a second cup of coffee and a quick look through the help-wanted ads to get the feel of what was available.

That brought her down. Hard. My God! she thought, feeling herself downsliding. I can't do anything. I can't type. I can't even file. Looking the way I do, I couldn't possibly even be a receptionist. I'd hate working in a factory, anything like that. Or a restaurant. She glanced at the waitress who, she saw, was staring at Sidonie's hands.

19

"Have an accident, hon?" the waitress asked with a gentle smile."

She looked down. Her hands looked terrible. Starting to scab. "Yes," she said. "Glass. A window."

"Yuwanna take care. Some athose look to be gettin' infected."

Sidonie stared at her hands as if she'd never seen them before. "You're right," she said, amazed by the number of cuts she saw. "I'll have to get some antiseptic. Thank you."

"Lookin' for a job, uh?" The waitress smiled again, refilling Sidonie's cup. "Lousy time to be lookin' with the inflation, what-have-you. My old man's laid off close on five months now. Hard on him, you know. Rough on a man having to stand around collectin' unemployment."

Sidonie glanced down at her now-filled cup, saying, "Thank you."

"Take care, hon," the waitress chirped, carrying the Pyrex pot down the counter.

Laying a dollar bill beside her untouched coffee, Sidonie left the coffee shop and returned to her car. For some reason, the waitress's concern made her want to cry. A total stranger had seemed more interested in her in the space of twenty minutes than Frank had in years.

She drove into the city, lifted as always by the sight of familiar old buildings, familiar old streets; heading into the center of town to the first address on her short list. On the fringes of Remington Park. Her favorite area of the city. An expensive, old area; the one-time nucleus of the city's very rich. Now the impressive houses were split up, sectioned-off into apartments, a few still privately owned by the very rich.

During her years in high school, she and Leslie Browning used to walk Leslie's Irish Setter, Beethoven, down to the Park, speculating on the houses and who lived in them.

She wondered about Leslie and what had become of her. I'll have to find out. I always liked Leslie. And Sally Endicott. Dinah. I used to have friends. What happened to them? Not even Christmas cards anymore. She passed the street where Leslie had lived and felt a gripping pang of nostalgia, recalling how the two of them had walked along the streets with Beethoven straining against the leash. Leslie had made a big-deal ceremony of allowing Sidonie to take temporary charge of the attention-getting, splendidly groomed setter.

I married Frank and surrendered my friends like my personal charge plates I had to give up, allowed myself to be fitted in with Frank's friends because it was expected. But I never really found the right fit. The thought of Frank's friends gave her a claustrophobic feeling. His friends. Where are mine? She tried to think—scouting the perimeter of the Park for a place to park the car—of one person who might fall into the category of "her friend." She couldn't think of one. All couples. All friends of Frank's. I have no friends, she thought, backing into a very tight space. I'll have to see if I can't get in touch with some of my old friends. I must have some left somewhere. They can't all have moved away. Not all of them.

"Writer and his wife lived here," the woman explained, showing Sidonie through the apartment. "Lovely folks. Just lovely. A teacher she was. Prettiest little thing y'ever wanna see. Died a few years back. He stayed on. 'Til last week. He moved out."

"She died?" Sidonie asked distractedly, moving through the rooms. Two bedrooms. What on earth could she do with two bedrooms?

"Cancer. Sad. Young woman, too."

Sidonie wasn't listening. She was too involved in the apartment, appreciating the brightness of the spacious living room, the charm of the master bedroom with its adjoining bathroom, the potential usefulness of the smaller second bedroom.

"Ad only came out in this morning's paper," the woman explained. "You're first. Very reasonable rent, considerin' the area."

"How much?"

"Two seventy-five. Won't find a thing around here for that. Not with two bedrooms, two bathrooms. Newly painted. Floors just done. I was you, I'd snap it up."

"Yes. Yes, I will."

"You'll take it? Two-year lease, you know. First and last month's rent, a month's security."

"When could I move in?"

"Any time you like. You married?"

"Y . . . No. I'm getting divorced." The words

were easy enough to say. But the feeling was devastating. As if she were the sole survivor of some terrible tragedy. "I could move in today? This afternoon?"

"What about your furniture?" the woman asked.

"I'll have to get some, I guess. I have a few things. I'll get the rest."

"Well, okay. You might as well come on downstairs while I get the lease ready. You wanna cuppa tea?"

Sidonie looked at her finally. A pleasant face.

"Thank you. I'd like a cup of tea."

Downstairs to the woman's tidy but cluttered apartment. Boston ferns, African violets lining the window sills. A smell of damp soil, growing things. Warm. Cozy.

"I'm divorced, too," she volunteered. "Eleven years. Sonofabitch took off with some kid, just left me high 'n' dry with an eight-year-old. Lucky thing for me I got this job. Otherwise, I'd of starved to death. Sonofabitch."

"Boy or girl?" Sidonie asked, sitting at the old-fashioned wooden kitchen table.

"Boy. He's off to college in a coupla weeks." She smiled proudly. "What's your name, anyhow? Mine's Aurora. Damnedest name, eh? That was my mom all over the place, givin' me a highfalutin' la-de-da name like Aurora."

"Sidonie . . . Graham. I suppose I'll start using my maiden name again."

"Sidney?"

23

"Sidonie. It sounds similar, but spelled S-I-D-O-N-I-E."

Aurora laughed. "Musta had one a those kinda mothers, too."

Sidonie laughed with her. It felt odd, as if it was something she hadn't done in years. The facial muscles protesting this unexpected exercise. "Sounds that way, doesn't it?" I'm going to like you, she decided, guessing at Aurora's age. Forty or thereabouts. "Tell me about the couple who lived here, the woman who died."

"I'll tell ya, it was sad." Aurora placed a cup of tea in front of Sidonie along with a box of shortbread. "Nicest couple you'd ever want to meet. From the looks of it, they didn't tell a living soul she was sick. I'd see her toward the end there, you know, sittin' over to the Park. Just sittin', watchin' the kids playing. Smiling, always talkin' to the kids. Then, next thing anybody knows, she's off to the hospital. One day she's rushing off to school—did I say she was a teacher?—smiling, so friendly. Next day, school's over and she's off to the park most afternoons.. Then' bingo! She's dead."

"What about the husband?"

"Went to live in England. Has a daughter, grandchildren over there. Lived right here in this building close on twenty years, he did. Came at first with the daughter. Then, later on married up with that one." Aurora sipped thoughtfully at her tea. "Tell you how nice she was. I sat down here and cried like a baby when I heard. Still think of her sometimes, see her in my mind, like, sittin' over to the Park. Well," she cleared her throat. "So much for that. Lemme go get those leases. I can fill 'em out while we're sittin'.'"

She left the room and Sidonie sat drinking the tea, trying to form a picture of the couple. She couldn't. All she could think was that she wanted to live in this place. She'd have someone she might talk to occasionally. And a nice place to live. I'm doing all right, she thought. I'm going to get through this. You're not going to kill me off, Frank.

"Lissen," Aurora said, returning with several copies of a lease. "There's a whole loada stuff downstairs you might wanna have. Been left over the years by tenants. You know?"

"That might be very good."

"You can have a look after we get you all signed on the dotted line and so forth. Just gotta fill in this crap. Hate this part of it," she sighed. "But there's only twelve apartments and they don't change hands all that often. Matter of fact, this is the first vacancy in close on three years. Thank God! And the landlord's a nice fella. That's important, you know."

"I suppose it is."

"Any kids?"

Sidonie shook her head.

"Better that way, you ask me. Less hassles. Well, might as well get these signed and outa the way." She pushed the forms across the table.

Without more than a glance at the amount for rent and various deposits, Sidonie signed her name at the bottom of each copy of the lease, then wrote out a check for eight hundred and twenty-five dollars. While writing the check, the thought came to her that she had no idea what she was doing. She simply knew she had to get away from that house, away from where it had all happened. Like a fugitive, she thought humorlessly. On the run. Looking for a safe hiding place.

Aurora studied the signature on the check, then folded it neatly, separated the copies of the lease and passed one over to Sidonie. "I guess you wanna have a look downstairs now, see if there's anything you'd be able to use."

"Oh, yes. Please."

Aurora studied the younger woman, deciding it was none of her business so she wouldn't go asking a whole bunch of questions. Easier 'n hell to go puttin' people off that way, asking a whole lot of questions. She did think, though, that this Sidney might be real good-looking if she wasn't so fat. Go figure people! she thought, leading the way to the basement.

Aurora took great pains to look her best. Kept an eye on her weight, had her hair done once a week and shopped around the good thrift shops for expensive, scarcely worn castoffs. Bad enough she had to be a glorified janitor. Damned if she'd look like one.

This one, she thought, looks more like a janitor than I do. Go figure it! Got the money to sit down and write out a big check like that. You got the money to do that, you got the money for doin' something about how you look.

There was an old, ornate headboard against the

far wall of the storage room. Sidonie made her way toward it wishing the light were better.

"This is beautiful," she said, turning to look at Aurora. "Does it belong to anyone?"

"You, if you want it. Been down here must be ten years. There's a footboard, slats around somewhere, too. Have to buy a mattress and box-spring, though."

"Oh, that's all right. I really would love to have this."

"I'll get Abe to bring it up for you. Abe's the handyman. You need a washer on the tap, or anything broken upstairs, you call me, I'll send Abe."

It was like a dream, Sidonie thought, looking through the discards in the storeroom. She found a table, badly stained and scratched. But with stripping and a fresh coat of varnish, it would do nicely as a bedside table. She also found a stately old armchair with a wide, curving back and rolled arms.

"These are wonderful things!" she exclaimed. "I can't believe no one wants them."

"Plain amazing what's junk to some folks, treasures to others," Aurora observed, as Sidonie moved around. "You just go ahead and pick out whatever you like. I'll be glad of the extra space."

In the end, she also opted to have a faded Oriental rug, an oak coatrack hidden beneath countless layers of paint, a round pedestal occasional table and a green glass lamp. Aurora talked her into having a huge carton of odds and ends of cookware and dishes.

"Never know what'll come in handy," she said.

27

"What you don't want, Abe'll bring back down here. Leavin' clean, eh?"

"What?" Sidonie looked up.

"Not plannin' on taking anything you didn't go in with."

"That's right," Sidonie said firmly. "Only what's mine."

"Me," Aurora said. "I got the lot. The whole dump, fulla twenty-year-old overstuffed crap. One a these days, I'm gonna get rid a the whole kit and caboodle and get me some a that nice Scandinavian stuff."

Sidonie left there with a set of keys and the first real sense of accomplishment she'd had in years. She drove downtown to Hamilton's to order a mattress and box-spring and a sofa, as well as shower curtains, burnt-bamboo shades for the apartment's many windows, two Ege Rya area rugs that would coordinate well with the colors of the old Oriental.

Then she drove back to the suburbs and started sorting through the things in the house. Methodically. I have to be fair, she told herself. No matter what kind of dirty, unfair tactics he uses. So she took half the sheets, blankets and towels. Half the dishes and pots and silver service. She found several cartons in the cellar, filled them and carried them out to the car. Glad of her old station wagon, she maneuvered things around so that she was able to take her rocker, a lamp she had chosen herself, two small tables that had come from her old bedroom at home, and the ten-inch portable color set.

Let *him* live with the antique black and white monster!

By the time she finished, the car was absolutely crammed, including the front seat and the well on the passenger side. With that fugitive feeling pressing her again, she got into the car and drove to the city. To her new home.

By eight that night, she'd made three trips back and forth. The house looked somewhat denuded without her books. (Frank's books consisted of one on contract bridge, several computer manuals, and an interoffice telephone directory.) But it was still a house filled with furniture, and her new apartment was a jumble of boxes and books and clothing all dumped in the middle of the living room.

Driven by some compulsive interior force, she began hanging away her clothes. She created tidy rows of books, filling the built-in cases in the living room and bit by bit reducing the accumulation of articles in the middle of the room.

With each item that came away from the mass and was settled somewhere, she felt more and more pleased with herself and more and more desperate. The desperation pulsed in her temples, sent perspiration streaming down her body and kept her moving. At eleven she realized she'd eaten nothing all day and went out to the car to drive to a still-open restaurant outside the Park for a hurried hamburger and coffee. Her stomach cramped after the first few bites but she finished the tasteless food and the acrid coffee before hurrying back to the apartment to stow away the kitchenwares.

Two A.M., and she couldn't make one more move. Her body refused.

She slept that night atop several folded blankets. In her new bedroom. The first time in her life she'd spent an entire night in a place entirely her own. Despite the turmoil inside her head, despite the urgency that forced her to set the alarm for an early hour so that she'd be up and able to finish clearing the living room, she felt good about what she'd accomplished so far. Still desperate. But pleased.

Screw you, Frank, she thought, fingers trembling as she switched off her new green glass lamp.

TWO

She was stiff, sore everywhere when she awakened the next morning. She sat up and leaned back against the wall, pulling the blankets up around her neck, staring at the far wall. Depression was there waiting for her and she fell into it the way she used to dive from the board of the family swimming pool as a kid. Whoom. All the way in.

I'm insane. What am I doing here? No pictures on the walls. Nothing covering the windows. The smell of fresh paint and floor wax and nowhere to put anything. He forced me to do this. I might not have done any of this if he hadn't reacted that way, insisting nobody could walk out on him. But it's going to be all right. I wanted to leave. I just didn't think . . . I thought somehow we'd talk about it, that he'd want to talk me out of leaving. But he didn't consider me suitably equipped for conversation, not even then. You don't talk to the hired help. Unreimbursed hired help. You don't talk to slaves. You simply issue orders.

She threw off the blankets and got up. Crouching, she got past the uncurtained windows and went into the bathroom. The shower made her feel better. Hot, hot to untie some of the body knots and ease away a little of the depression. Some coffee. Thank God she'd remembered to bring the coffee pot. But no sugar. No cream. I hate black coffee! She drank it, but it tasted like boiled, flavored water.

She carried her cup out to the living room, cheered by the still-pleasing dimensions of the room and the book-filled cases. She set the cup down on the floor and started putting away the remainder of the books. They filled almost the whole wall.

"Good!" she said aloud, retrieving her cup, heading out to the kitchen for more coffee.

She could not sustain these temporary surges of self-satisfaction when they came. The idea that Frank wasn't going to allow her to get away with this returned insistently, like a stray, starved dog to a back door where food had been once given.

I can't stay inside here all day. I'll give in, become frightened, start gearing myself up for another defeat. I've put everything away. The living room floor, dry-mopped, is shining, pristine. I must not sit here and look at the walls. I'll go crazy. God, how do people live alone? How do they fill up the days, the nights? What am I supposed to do in here all by myself?

All at once, she knew where she'd go and wondered why she hadn't thought of it sooner. Aunt Claudia. She felt cheered just thinking about her aunt.

God! Somewhere to go. Someone to see who doesn't belong to Frank. *My* aunt. And close enough to walk to. I haven't walked in eight years, she realized, distributing her things in the bathroom medicine cabinet. Eight years. There weren't any sidewalks for walking. Nobody walks in the suburbs. You don't go anywhere on foot. Drive here, drive there. To think when I first got that car I'd beg the family to send me on errands just so I could get behind the wheel and start all that power going.

"First really intelligent move you've made in far too long!" Claudia said, lighting one of her Sobranie cigarettes with the black paper and gold filter. "I'm surprised, truthfully, Sidonie, you've stayed with that dreary man as long as you have."

"You never told me you thought he was dreary."

"Really, darling." Claudia smiled. "One doesn't go about pronouncing other people's husbands dreary, saying straight out what one thinks of them. It'd be frightfully costly in terms of friendships, associations one values. You look a bit stunned, Sidonie. Are you quite sure you know what you're doing?"

"I'm not quite sure about anything. I just have the feeling I've done something right. And I'm not even sure what it is I've done. I don't know. I feel as if I'm running standing still."

"Have you thought at all about what you're going to do?" Claudia asked.

"I'm having trouble thinking."

"I think it's exciting, actually. One doesn't have all that many opportunities to make fresh starts."

Claudia crossed her somewhat too-short, slightly bowed legs and smoothed her rose-colored crepe skirt over her knees. "There must be something you're good at. Isn't there?"

"I can't think of anything," Sidonie said, examining her lacerated hands.

"Of course you can do things! What was the point of your education if you can't at age twenty-nine, *do* something?"

"For instance?"

"You could work as a salesclerk. All sorts of stores about, you know. And I trust you have a little something put by."

"I took all the money from the savings account."

"Good for you! I *am* proud of you! Now, if you have a bit of money put by, why not go downtown to one of the nicer shops and apply for a job? They always, it seems to me, need higher-caliber sales-people. You can't sit about biting your nails all day, every day. Do stop that, Sidonie! It's an outward sign of the onslaught of interior decay."

"He had to make the moment his. Had to take a position and strike back. He said I was fat and lazy."

"You *are* a wee bit on the hefty side," Claudia said, exhaling a thick stream of smoke before carefully crushing out her cigarette. "Any mirror would show you that. As to lazy, I couldn't say now, could I? And it's certainly easy enough to remedy being fat. Diet. Get yourself this super book on yoga I use. Marvelous, yoga. Tighten you up like a drum, put everything back where it's supposed to be."

Sidonie looked at her aunt, marveling as she always did. Fifty-six. Widowed almost five years. Still bleaches her hair, has her nails manicured. Wears the damnedest clothes and custom-made shoes. Has always laughingly referred to herself as lapsed peerage. Breasts out to there, but a trim little figure. Not pretty but always gives the impression of being much more than merely pretty with big, meticulously made-up blue eyes and a complexion I'd give anything to have. "How the hell do you do it?" Sidonie asked admiringly.

"Self-respect," Claudia said seriously. "You've been lacking, Sidonie. Honestly! Doesn't it matter to you that you look . . . I don't think I can *describe* how you look. You were the loveliest looking child. Poor Elizabeth must be having a seizure, wherever she is. When I think of how she fussed over your clothes, over the way you looked, trotting you off to beauty salons at the age of six or whenever. You can't be happy with all this, can you?"

"Of course I'm not happy!"

"You're not unintelligent, Sidonie. You've made the first moves. Now keep on with it. Whatever you do, don't go crawling back because you find it difficult to adjust initially. *Do* for yourself. Have your hair done, a facial, steambath, massage. Do it all! You'll feel superb and get a good start in the right direction. Buy yourself some smashing new clothes. No! Do something about dieting first. Then, as a reward, treat yourself to an entirely new wardrobe. Take yourself out for a skinny little dinner at a good restaurant. Go to the cinema, the theater.

Don't become trapped by your decision! You've made it, now keep moving."

"I have moved into town."

"Very good! Where?"

"Outside the Park. I found an apartment, moved in yesterday."

"And I suppose you need bits and bobs and want to go poking about in the attic." Claudia smiled knowingly.

"Could I?" Sidonie brightened. She'd always loved Aunt Claudia's attic, and had spent what seemed like most of her childhood up there pretending she was someone Louisa May Alcott had written.

"Carry on! I'm not in the least interested in climbing all those stairs. Just check with me before you go carting off all my things."

Claudia studied Sidonie's eyes closely for several seconds before saying, "You haven't mentioned your feelings." She smiled again. "You're a little demented at the moment but I get the decided impression you're very proud of yourself."

"I am, a little. Maybe a lot. I didn't plan it, you know. Suddenly, I was just at the end and I couldn't go any further. Now I've got the jitters. It's hard to explain. I have to have some time to think about how I feel. May I go up to the attic now?"

"One word of advice, my darling. Whatever you do, don't go flying off into another marriage. It'd be the worst possible thing you could do. Move about. This is a fine chance for you to do some finding out about yourself. You married far too young. I've always thought so, told you so. Now you've made a decision, a good one, and you've all sorts of future in front of you. Don't be a fool and hurry into another marriage because you're frightened. Believe me! I know you haven't had time to come to terms with your decision, haven't yet realized the full implications of what you've done. But you will. And it won't be easy. It'll be bloody difficult, but very worthwhile. You're losing *nothing*, leaving Frank."

"You really can't stand him, can you?"

"Never could!" Claudia declared, chin uplifted. "I frankly can't see how you could either, with your background. I haven't any prejudices to do with ethnic origins, Sidonie. But a peasant's a peasant, no matter how you disguise him. And that man was a prince among peasants. Any man who would wear white socks and brown shoes to his wedding is a peasant."

Sidonie laughed until she thought she'd cry. Claudia lit a fresh cigarette, pleased with the response her comments had generated.

"You're right," Sidonie admitted, wiping her eyes with a Kleenex. "A peasant. I love you, Aunt Claudia." The laughter abruptly threatened to turn to sobbing. "You've always been so hideously truthful. Do you think that I've done all this too late?"

"Do *you* think so?"

"I don't know what I think. About anything. I feel as if being married to Frank I learned how not to think. There's a me inside somewhere but I can't remember who she is or how she feels. I don't know. I'd better go up to the attic now."

Claudia agreed, after a minimum of token bickering, to let Sidonie take two family portraits, several decrepit chairs and a mirror.

"Think of it as the beginning of your life," Claudia said as Sidonie was leaving. "Take small steps, go slowly. It will all come to you in time. I'm always here when you need me. And do be sure to let me know when you've a telephone."

How do I feel? she asked herself that evening, sitting in the as-yet unrecovered armchair from the storeroom in the basement, staring at the TV set.

I feel, now that I've talked to Aunt Claudia, as if somehow I've managed—after eight years—to locate myself, reestablish a sort of fundamental contact with myself. And I feel so mad I could knock down a brick wall with my bare hands. Mad. I'd like to break every bone in your stinking body, Frank. Hot-stuff computer programmer. People programmer. A crafty peasant with a gift for stealing the spotlight. Always dissatisfied with me in little ways. Never saying so, letting little looks speak for you. A program carefully computed to keep me in my place. The place you designated. I saw it but kept refusing to be aware, really aware. Being aware would've meant having to face too many things all at once.

And what was I? Some kind of obedient slave, scurrying around trying to do it all the way you liked. Because pleasing you was the program. Twice a week lovemaking regular as clockwork that wasn't ever anywhere near what I expected it to be. You reduced me in every way. And my brain finally rejected the input.

Thinking about making love with Frank brought on a spasm of revulsion. All your little signals, like some idiot boy scout in the back of somebody's borrowed car. That was the feeling. Coughing a certain way to let me know. Scratching my back. And always ended too soon.

And you wouldn't let me have a child. Now I'm so glad. God, glad! I'd be in big trouble right now with a child. I wouldn't have dared leave with a child.

No more dinners to cook. No more jockey shorts, shirts to iron, socks. Picking up after you. I'll buy a scale, weigh myself daily. Go to the hairdresser, have my hair trimmed, wear it down the way I used to. Get a lawyer. Claudia's bound to know a lawyer. She knows a good half of the people in this city. I won't come back, Frank. Don't wait for me, don't expect me!

She got up and turned off the TV set. Why the hell am I sitting here watching television? No more of that. All that's finished. There's no food in this place. I'll go shopping. For food *I* like, for a change. I can do anything. Can't I?

She went down to the car and drove miles outside the city to a shopping center that stayed open until midnight where she bought cleaning items for the apartment and very carefully selected nonfattening foods, ignoring the hunger pains in her stomach that shrieked at her to grab for cookies and dough-

39

nuts and squidgy-looking loaves of white bread. Stupid to go grocery shopping when you're hungry. You want to open your mouth and eat the entire supermarket. I have to lose a lot of weight, get back to looking like myself again. Metrecal cookies and sugar-free drinks. I'll start from the outside and work my way in. Sit-ups and whatever else is in the yoga book. I can do it. Exercise half the day and night if I want to; watch the TV shows *I* like; sleep on the side of the bed *I* prefer; eat what *I* like. I'll miss the washer and dryer, though, and the dishwasher. I didn't even ask Aurora about laundry. There must be a laundry room.

She could easily have eaten six of everything, but forced herself to settle for tuna salad with lettuce and two cups of tea without sugar, and went to bed with some of the desperation dissipated and hunger pains she struggled to ignore.

The next morning, she went downstairs to use Aurora's telephone to arrange for an installation, then to call Aunt Claudia for the name of a lawyer.

"If I'm not back in time, could you let the telephone man in?" she asked Aurora.

"Oh, sure. You like the place, eh?"

"I love it. I may stay forever. Thank you for letting me use your phone. I'll give you dinner one night, to repay you."

"Take you up on it." Aurora laughed, reaching inside her dress to pull up her bra strap. "I get so sick of my own cooking, I could die."

Downtown again to Hamilton's to the book department to buy the yoga book, on upstairs to get a scale. On her way out of the store, she bought her once-favorite perfume and some dusting powder too. Frank claimed it made him sneeze, so she'd given it up.

She stopped at a hardware store to buy steel wool, paint, brushes, paint remover, rubber gloves. She'd refinish that little table for the bedroom. Do that first.

Having skipped breakfast, she ate two crackers and drank a cup of black coffee for lunch and worked through the afternoon, stripping the old varnish from the table. The telephone installer arrived at four-fifteen and within minutes had one phone hooked up in the bedroom and an extension in the living room. The outlets were already there. He was in and out so fast she couldn't even offer him a Coke.

The table was stripped clean. She replaced the top on the tin of remover and went out to the kitchen to prepare her first skinny dinner. Asparagus, lean broiled steak, salad. She ate very slowly, turning the pages of the illustrated yoga exercise book. Ninety minutes after eating. The book advised against commencing the exercises any sooner.

So, still ravenously hungry but determined not to give in to it, she watched Walter Cronkite (I'm not hungry, I am not hungry), reassured by the sane-looking, sane-sounding sameness of the man; finding herself painfully (Why? she wondered) choked up when he said, "And that's the way it is, June twenty-fourth, 1975. This is Walter Cronkite for CBS News. Goodnight."

Like a damned fool, she croaked, "Good night, Walter," smiling through a murk of tears as she got up to turn off the set. A fool maybe. But it meant something. No one to make snide comments on her overburdened sentimentality.

For the next hour, she oiled and polished and painstakingly cleaned the ornately carved bedstead, stepping back finally to admire her work. I love this bed. It's *mine*.

Time for the exercises. In front of the mirror she'd been given by Aunt Claudia. In the nude to shame herself into doing every last exercise down to perfection. No cheating. No skipping. For thirty-six minutes until her heart was racing, she was soaking wet and could scarcely catch her breath. A hot shower and into the bedroom for her second night on the blankets. I hope that mattress comes soon. I may not be too old for fresh starts, but I'm definitely too old for sleeping on the floor.

In the dark, battling off thoughts of ice cream sundaes, peanut butter sandwiches, she ran her hands over her body. It's all coming off, she promised herself. How can I be anything, anyone if I don't look like the me I used to know? When I can't grab anything, not one half inch of skin, I'll know I'm getting there. Where? God! For what? Somewhere. It's strange, hard work getting used to sleeping alone. Keep telling yourself this was what you wanted.

The next morning she awakened to the sound of

a telephone. Her first call. It was Frank.

"Where the hell are you?" Frank demanded. "And what d'you think you're doing taking all my money? You can't do that!"

"I can. I've already done it. You get the house, I get the money. That's fair."

"And what in hell d'you do to the kitchen window?" he went on, airing his list of grievances. "There's glass all over the goddamned place."

"I smashed it," she said, feeling shaky, feeling scared. He might know some new words to use, some new ploy to lure her back. "I felt like it. Anything else?"

"Don't think you can just come waltzing back here," he warned. "Nobody walks out on me."

"I've done it," she said evenly. "Somebody's walked out on you."

"You drunk, Sid? You sound drunk."

"Go to hell, Frank! You'll hear from my lawyer." She slammed down the receiver and burst into angry tears, unable to understand that substance inside that cowered, cringing at the sound of his angry voice.

I have a right to be doing what I'm doing. I won't allow you to intimidate me. Your gambit didn't work. I'm not going to come back to you— not any way at all, not crawling or waltzing. Not coming back. It doesn't matter if I'm scared or confused. The only thing I know is I'm not ever coming back. There has to be something more for me. More than obedient acquiescence, more than rarely questioning agreement. More.

After the first week, the days began to develop a pattern revolving around battling her craving for food, exercising, moving things here and there in the apartment and imagining various means of retaliation Frank might seek to employ. But when time passed and he made no more phone calls and silence seemed to blanket her actions, muffling them yet amplifying the groans of her exertion, she became partially relieved and somehow more frightened. She couldn't believe he was just going to let it all happen. Maybe there really was another woman and he had been readying himself to tell her.

While she stretched and strained and grappled with her hunger, she blamed him for any number of things. Her horrible appetite, her house-trained habits, her loss of status, her dreadful loneliness and her unanticipated state of physical withdrawal.

Nightly, she lay in bed agonizingly aware of the broadening implications of living alone. And though she was angry with Frank for his failing to provide her with the kind of heightened and romantic satisfaction she'd always privately craved, she was nevertheless surprised to find herself aching for the purely animal comfort of a body beside hers; yearning for holding, touching, someone to bump into in the night. It seemed the very worst aspect of her escape: living untouched, unloved in the very simplest ways. No embraces, no caresses, no sharing.

It was in this area that the greatest temptation lay. Go back to Frank. Choke on pride and creep back, head bowed, abject. No. She resented him for indirectly casting her into a state of hungry desperation. Yet, within this state, her determination to redo herself, her life, all of her, grew until her focus was entirely fixed on the attainment of both a new external image and a kind of independence she felt would be infinitely preferable to the domesticated bondage she'd known with Frank.

In her thoughts she was many different things. Too often, she felt like a defenseless child; uninformed of worldly ways, unequipped to cope with or understand them. She'd donned wedded blinders eight years earlier and somehow they'd managed to become embedded in her flesh. Removing them was painful. The sudden glare of life's realities was almost blinding.

She was also an Amazon, Wonder Woman, Gloria Steinem and Bella Abzug. She reduced Frank to near-ashes, to flailing, whimpering jelly. His manly disguises, his preferential demands were stripped away (by her incisive, cutting comments) and thrown to one side, leaving the pale-fleshed, imperfect male body quivering under the cold, articulate blast of her retroactive anger.

There was to be no contest. Frank did not, according to his lawyer, wish to argue matters. He didn't want her back. The divorce would be granted after a ninety-day waiting period. That simple. That devastating. She'd expected more of a battle. Something more. But it was all very businesslike. The two lawyers spoke on the telephone, arrived at an alimony figure, discussed who'd taken what, agreed it was equitable and that was that.

"He's agreed to give you three hundred a month," her lawyer told her.

She nodded like a puppet, thinking, It's not enough. I want more. Not money. Money didn't matter. No. What she wanted was some sort of humbled apology; a bended-knee monologue of contrition. Words. She wanted Frank down there on his knees admitting he'd wasted eight years of her life, admitting he was sorry about the shabby qualities of their relationship. She wouldn't get any of that. Yet she was getting what she'd wanted. Wasn't she?

She submissively nodded her head to everything the lawyer said, thinking, He's done it again: robbed me for the last time of satisfaction in a venture. She told herself she'd have to stop thinking that way. She'd have to because in ninety days it would all be over. For good. Permanently. Ended.

Three months. It didn't sound like a long time, but it seemed to last forever. Ninety days to brood and sweat and starve and fume; to imagine Frank rolling around in bed with some faceless woman, performing all those intricate sexual acts upon the face and body of this featureless creature that he'd never deigned to perform upon Sidonie. It rankled, made her skin feel hard as cement, made her insides roil, made her talk aloud to herself as she paced the floor of her apartment trying to convince herself she'd won and never mind that Frank hadn't come pleading, begging her to return. Why, she wondered, did she want that when she didn't want Frank? Why did she mourn the absence of telephone calls, conversations meant to induce her to come home?

Lonely. Not in the days that went too quickly. But in the hours after sundown when the apartment seemed far too large, the corners too dark and shadowy, her hands too empty. Sitting down to stare at TV, then getting up to go in search of something only to fail to remember, upon arriving at her destination (in kitchen, bedroom or bathroom) what she'd come after in the first place. Turning, turning. To stare at blank spaces on the walls, thinking blankly. Of something to fill the blank spot, of something to put inside herself to ease the ache. Lonely. Thinking about going out— for a meal, to see a movie, to take a walk. But too trapped inside her convoluted thoughts to make a move. Dragging herself heavily through each evening hour, telling herself, I've won, but finding the words pointless, empty. Won what?

Claudia came at the end of the first month's waiting to say, "You have done well, darling. Now, this place has character. You were jolly lucky to find it. And I must say I do like your decor."

She pushed Sidonie over to the windows to scrutinize Sidonie's face in stark daylight, humming and yessing to herself while her large eyes moved calculatingly over Sidonie's face for what felt like hours before saying, "There's a face emerging here I recognize. You're doing well. How much have you lost?"

"Twelve pounds."

"Wonderful! Keep on with it! You're beginning

to take form. You must remember never to allow people to witness a lack of self-respect. They see it and any potential interest in you dies on the vine. Desperation drives people into the hills, Sidonie. So, be the best. Do it to the hilt! Out there," she flung out her arm dramatically, "there's a world filled with men. Please don't go out with the hope of finding a new one as fast as you can. Someone to stake a claim on. Go out and enjoy what they *can* give you and don't fret about the things they can't. You may learn, in the process, what you have to give. There's definitely something," Claudia said earnestly. "You have something, Sidonie. I'm getting the sense of it. I can't quite pin it down as yet. But I will. I will. I'd always hoped you were simply slow."

"What are you talking about?"

Claudia softened, seeing the confusion clinging to Sidonie's features.

"I'm the one, darling, who always seems to say the things others think but rarely say. When I was younger, it dropped me square in the middle of more embarrassing situations than I'd care to describe. But the fact of the matter is I am truthful. You're well out of that marriage. I'm delighted that you had the strength to make a decision and you're seeing it through. It isn't easy. I know. Just remember you've given up little. Nothing. The only reason Frank pursued you in the first place was because of your long driveway."

"What?" Sidonie smiled.

"Think of where you lived! Then think of where

Frank came from. He was in love with the fact that the driveway to that house on Simpson Hill was a good quarter-mile long. And not only did he make it all the way up the driveway, he got through the front door and beyond, to you. He always was one of the worst sort of opportunists. The sort who think they'll elevate themselves through a clever marriage. I do wish you'd work on your perspectives, darling. He wasn't particularly nice or particularly clever nine years ago when he began courting you with his clean-cut college-boy ways. He's certainly no nicer or cleverer now. A small man with a small brain. Whereas you, Sidonie, are a woman with potential. I was beginning to abandon hope but this move has entirely restored my faith. I blame your mother as much as I blame anyone. Encouraging that lout out of typical, preposterous pseudo-liberal notions. The only thing that would have pleased her more than your marrying Frank would have been if Frank had been coal black."

"Claudia!" Sidonie began to laugh.

"Quite true!" she said confidently. "Fine with me if you fancy black men. I've seen some positively gorgeous blacks in my time with a good deal more going for them than Frank ever had. Which is beside the point. The point is: you wanted to get away from that house. I can't say I blame you for that. But you didn't fight terribly hard for your freedom. Frank was available. Your mother approved. So in you leaped. A mistake, Sidonie. Never mind, though! I'm more and more convinced you were simply a latent type. The sort who suddenly takes shape and begins to grow later on; the sort who becomes better and better with age. Honestly! Look at you! Even now you look better than I've ever seen you look. Take off your dress!"

Sidonie laughed. "Are you out of your mind?"

"There's something I want to see. Do it!"

"You're some kind of lunatic sexist!"

"Nonsense! Come along! I haven't all day. I have a dinner date this evening. If you expect me to help and advise you, I have to know what we're working with. Good breasts are a great blessing, you know. You simply cannot imagine the number of times I considered having mine surgically reduced. When I was much younger, of course."

Feeling like a fool, wondering why she could never seem to say no, Sidonie unzipped her dress. Like a schoolgirl at the nurse's office, color rushing into her face. All fumbling fingers and useless hands, total embarrassment. She stepped out of the dress and suffered Claudia's critical visual inspection.

"Get yourself some good-looking lingerie, for a start," Claudia said, eyes narrowed. "That was half the reason for my asking. Good skin tone, though. Breasts are still too big," she said appraisingly, "but they'll go down as you lose more weight. Good. Thank you."

"Gigi's grandmother," Sidonie mumbled. Dismissed from the inspection, struggling back into her dress. Feeling oddly gratified at the approval. And proud that the sweat and hunger were producing satisfactory results.

"Come sit down," Claudia said, extracting a Sobranie from her bag, lighting it with an engraved gold Dunhill. "I'm going to give you another piece of advice. Take it the way it's intended, Sidonie," she cautioned. "Help yourself get through this. Work off some of the accumulating tension. You're so on edge it's difficult being with you just now. You're going to have to do something about it."

"For example?" Sidonie found herself becoming exasperated.

"What every little girl, teenager and grown woman does when there's no other available option. Must I be graphic?"

"You are really something!" Sidonie said with a shake of her head, caught midway between anger and surprise, not sure whether to love Claudia more for her accurate assumptions or to hate her for knowing.

"I'm realistic," Claudia countered. "You'll find I'm not wrong. And I do like the apartment. The bed's smashing! Wherever did you find it? And what was that oblique reference to someone's grandmother?"

"Oh, nothing. The bed was in the storeroom in the basement. Aurora let me take it. One of the former tenants left it."

"Who is Aurora?"

"She runs the building."

"Silly name," Claudia said dismissingly.

"So is Claudia."

"True," Claudia agreed unexpectedly. "There's a definite, rather nasty implication there that one's

parents would've preferred a male child. Sidonie
now, that's a very pretty name. But affected. My
sister was unforgivably affected. Always. Even as
a child. Airs and graces and living up to one's
station. Having a family like ours was like having
some sort of highly contagious rash. Far more of
a hindrance than a blessing. You should be grateful
for your father, Sidonie. Were it not for Lucas, I
doubt you'd have had any chance whatsoever. Certainly, you'd never have had the strength to take
any sort of a stand. I'm convinced his were the
dominant genes. And jolly lucky thing for you they
were! Would you have enjoyed being a replica of
your mother?"

"Why didn't you have any children?" Sidonie
asked. It was something she'd always questioned
but never given voice to.

Claudia, losing some of her insouciance, sucked
hard on her Sobranie, taking an inordinate amount
of time shaking the ash from the tip.

"Do you know what vaginal prolapse is?" Claudia
asked finally, her eyes on the ashtray.

"It sounds like everything collapses or something."

"Or something. It's repaired surgically. Look it
up sometime in a medical dictionary. You might
also, while you're about it, investigate the causes.
I must fly. I'm going to be late."

"I'm sorry," Sidonie said. "I didn't . . . I shouldn't
have . . ."

"Sidonie, I love you. You're self-pitying just
now and sometimes intentionally thick-headed. But
you've a good heart and a fine brain. My way of

helping may not be all you'd wish for but my intentions are the best. I'm not a sexist or a racist. Nor am I an eccentric. I've lived in the world, grown up in it. And, sadly, it's all too often a place where women are exploited and manipulated. Primarily because they're so conditioned to expect it they don't know any other way to function. I'm trying, in my erratic fashion, to decondition you. God knows I'm difficult and opinionated. But in this instance, I'm right. You're having a wretched time and I am trying, in whatever fashion I am able, to prod you out of a very destructive lethargy. You can't quit at this juncture, Sidonie! Not having come this far. You've far too much going for you. You're emerging as a beautiful woman. You've got a lovely figure. And a damned good brain. Keep it functioning! If you don't, you're going to find yourself being exploited and manipulated just as you were for the past eight years. Don't let it happen! It's terribly easy to allow it to happen. Don't! Use what you have. Find out what else you have. Be the best, expect the best. You may get it. Compromise of the sort you've been used to invariably leads to more and more compromise until you've lost whatever decisiveness and individuality you possessed to begin with. One needn't be dependent upon men for one's identity, Sidonie. You have an identity. Being alone, living alone. None of that makes you a social pariah. There's not a thing wrong with entering into a relationship if you're exercising a healthy awareness. But blindly dashing into something because you're seeking comfort, because you're not entirely certain you haven't made a terrible error is a form of sheer madness. Certain forms of comfort come only from one's self."

"You compromised in your marriage," Sidonie offered, a series of memory films flicking across an interior screen.

"There's compromise and compromise. When one does compromise in order to improve an already fruitful relationship, that's intelligent. When one compromises simply to hold someone's interest, it's self-deluding and somehow contemptible. Nothing can be all that one-sided. No good relationship is. There's no need for apologies. I've upset you equally. People who love each other do that. It happens. Now I really must fly."

"How do you know you're right?"

"Being right doesn't matter," Claudia said thoughtfully. "Whether I'm right or wrong about you will have no bearing on my future. Good advice may have a very positive bearing on yours. I know I sound like a frightful old know-it-all but all advice is hard to take, no matter the source. And this isn't a time for delicately selecting one's words. It isn't that sort of situation. Not what you need. You need truth. Honesty. My brand's a wee bit on the painful side but you wouldn't have come to me if you hadn't been seeking unadorned truth."

"You're right. I wouldn't have."

Claudia offered her cheek. Sidonie kissed her. And Claudia, in full control as always, went on her way.

THREE

In the course of that conversation, Claudia also said, "I keep expecting you to say something about love, Sidonie. But you don't. It seems to me in this sort of situation, the abandoned wife goes on and on endlessly about how much she *loves* the departed scoundrel. And how much, supposedly, he loved her. But not you, Sidonie. Not a blessed word. Which is why, my darling, I do not believe love is at issue here. I doubt it ever was."

Damn her anyway, Sidonie thought, walking her way through lunchtime in order to entirely bypass this too-tempting time of day, this most dangerous part of any day. One lousy carrot stick and she'd be off, telling herself just a little of this, a little of that and before she'd be able to stop herself, half the refrigerator's contents gone. No. It was mandatory to pretend lunchtime didn't exist. Between twelve and one was the *really* dangerous time. After that, a cup of hot tea at two or thereabouts would satisfy any craving for food and she'd be able to get through until six or six-thirty and dinner (her only meal of the day).

The amazing part of starving was that it worked. Actually worked. By six-thirty or seven, she'd have little appetite, if any. The first few bites of food would drop into her stomach with all the impact of miniature hydrogen bombs. Half or a quarter of the meal consumed, she dumped the rest into the garbage. Within half an hour, her body would be actively combatting the insanity she'd perpetrated upon it during the course of the day. Stomach cramps, frequent diarrhea. The net result being that by the end of the second month's waiting, she'd lost twenty-two pounds and nearly as many inches.

She measured her body with the same fixed intensity she'd once reserved for the preparation of elaborate meals. Measured everywhere. The tops of her arms, tops of her legs. Hips, waist, breasts, thighs, calves, neck. Everywhere a tapemeasure could be applied. Her hipbones showed, her abdomen grew flatter. Her body seemed to be the proving ground, the arena, the gallery where her successes were displayed, reflecting the success occurring inside.

The yoga, at which she was rapidly becoming proficient, left her exhausted, aglow with accomplishment and, in this area at least, altogether pleased with herself as she stood beneath the nightly, scalding shower.

While she twisted and stretched herself into Locusts, Cobras, back-bends, bows and various other of the prescribed positions, she considered

(a) her present circumstances, (b) her continuing anger, and (c) this issue of love.

At the time she'd met Frank, she'd thought she'd been in love. But how could you tell? Looking backward, her doubts were substantial. It hadn't been love, she decided, so much as an overwhelming desire to have more of those long, wet kisses that left her with impaired breathing and dampened underpants. Hugging, kissing, stroking, all the delicious preliminaries. That staggering anticipatory high stoked by the remembered admonitions that they'd feel differently about each other if they went all the way before marriage, lose respect for each other and be breaking some unwritten churchly commandment that ordered a girl to her bridal bed in a state of encapsulated, unblemished virginity. It was only later and indirectly—through remarks made by Aunt Claudia—that Sidonie came to understand just how archaic and passé her mother's standards were.

So they didn't. And fought about it. He accused her of ". . . giving me a swell case of blue balls." Her mouth formed a shocked O as she tried to imagine it.

She accused him of ". . . trying to make me do something I know we shouldn't do yet. If you really loved me, you'd understand and be willing to wait. It isn't easy for me either, you know."

Then, having stated their petulant cases, they'd do it all over again; racing through their ritual foreplay, each of them mentally groping for some swifter route to that bridal bed, each of them in a state of heated panic.

Foreplay, preliminaries, pleasure. That all ended with abrupt and stunning conclusiveness once they were finally married and she was available for constant and continued in-depth inspections.

Once he had legal claim to her, Frank seemed to lose all his imagination. If he'd ever possessed any. And along with it went her anticipation. Not all at once. But gradually, almost unnoticeably, over an extended period of time. He rarely seemed willing to give her either a chance to become involved or to want him. Make me want you, she'd tell him silently. Do something to make me want you. Show me. But he never did. He was in too much of a hurry to writhe his way toward ejaculation. Hurrying, hurrying.

The only times when their lovemaking wasn't just to satisfy him were when she'd either had so much to drink she required no preliminaries or when she'd been secretly devouring Frank's copies of *Penthouse* and *Playboy* and had managed to arouse herself to such a degree that she might have made love to almost anyone. But she made love with Frank, and went to sleep filled with fantasies inspired by the magazines. Unfulfilled.

Love?

If love was doing someone's laundry, dusting, vacuuming, cleaning the windows, cooking three-course dinners, then she'd loved him. If love was making a ceremony out of twice-monthly handing her a check for deposit to her bank account, if it

was regularly forgetting to comment on the food she
so slavishly prepared, if love was making a brave and
noble display of taking out the garbage and tend-
ing to the raking of leaves and mowing of grass, if
love was one-sided conversations about his work,
his office, his friends and rarely anything else, then
Frank had loved her.

Jesus! she thought, rolling over onto her back
to begin the slow, slow situps. That's not love. But
what the hell *is* it? And if that *isn't* love, what is?

She accomplished the situp, touched her toes and
abandoned the exercise. I have an *idea* what it is.
But what *is* it? How do you recognize it? The only
thing I'm sure I do know is that I don't love Frank.
And I don't think I ever did.

Claudia offered to accompany her on the day of
the hearing.

"Oh, you're *kind*," Sidonie said, deeply moved
by the offer. "But I think I've got to go this one
alone. I don't know. I just feel as if—I mean—I
went into this by myself, I should be able to come
out of it myself."

"Good for you! I do hope you've got something
smashing to wear."

"I'm on my way out now. I have an appointment
at Arden's, then I'm going shopping."

"You will remember to do something about your
hair, won't you darling? Don't let that lout see he's
made any points."

"I'm having it done."

"It's merely a formality, Sidonie," Claudia said

in a rare gentle tone of voice. "After tomorrow, it's a lovely new beginning."

The hairdresser made a terrific fuss, declaring, "You don't *know*! I have women come in here paying a fortune trying to get their hair this color. I've never *seen* a head of hair so perfect."

She snipped and trimmed, wet clumps of red hair scattered on the floor. "Not one bit kinky, either! God, *are* you *lucky*! I think we'll just blow it dry You're the type who looks good messy. Definitely!"

The makeup lady came over, looking very serious, murmuring to the hairdresser, the two of them possessively proud of Sidonie's naturally curly, thick, carrot-colored hair.

"Lots of eye makeup!" the makeup lady decided, taking over as the hairdresser brushed loose bits of hair off Sidonie's cape and neck with a brush as soft as eyelashes. "And with that skin, bright red lipstick. It'll be stunning! Sim-ply stunning!"

Oooing and aaahing over Sidonie's pasty, be-freckled face; a look of fiercely intense concentration on the overly made-up make-up woman. They always looked that way, Sidonie thought. As if they'd sampled every single one of the products they were pushing. All at one time.

"Transparent base. Always, sweets. Let the freckles show. They're di-vine! A lovely orangey blusher. And charcoal shadow on the lids, a bit of our Forest Green just above to bring out the contrast. God, isn't it classic? Classic!"

Her breath was surprisingly sweet, her skin pure and poreless like an infant's, her scent pleasurable as she patted and puffed and polished and dabbed, then turned the chair with a flourish, saying, "*There!*" as Sidonie was presented with the mirror image of a wind-blown redhead with upslanting green eyes and a wide, red mouth.

She laughed, elated. Her chest felt overfull—of air, laughter, fear.

"That's unbelievable!" She laughed, leaning closer to the mirror. "You have to show me how you did it. So I'll be able to."

"Easy as pie, sweets."

And only sixty-six seventy worth of cosmetics: base, transparent powder, blusher, eyeshadow (two shades), eyeliner, mascara, lipstick, lipstick pencil, lip gloss, moisturizer, under-eye cream. A treasure trove, a new paint-by-numbers face. And, at the local discount drugstore, a 1000-watt blow-dryer. To keep that perpetually windblown look working for her.

Then, hurrying to Hamilton's. Upstairs to the Better Dresses to try on sixes. No more thirteens. *Sixes.* Oh, God, I'm so happy! Size six! The saleslady highly complimentary, sharing the joy of Sidonie's new body.

Coming away with two, far too expensive pairs of beautifully fitting trousers with matching Shetland sweaters, a grass-green wraparound dress of fine, light wool, two skirts and four blouses. Knee-high suede boots from the Better Shoes. A white London Fog raincoat with belt for advertising a new, tiny waist and a slouch hat just for the hell of it.

"Aunt Claudia, come have dinner with me. You have to tell me what you think."

"Dinner date, darling. But we'll stop by on our way."

Claudia arrived, accompanied by an exceptionally handsome man in his late fifties. Gray-haired, dressed to a T, utterly picture-perfect dignified-sophisticated. (Aunt Claudia, I'm jealous.)

"This is Jacob. We'll be five minutes, Jacob." She smiled radiantly as she swept Sidonie off to the bedroom for an inspection check, pronouncing the clothes and the hair and the makeup, "Marvelous! Simply marvelous! How much have you lost, finally?"

"Twenty-six pounds." Sidonie grinned. "Size six. Can you believe it?"

"You're beautiful, Sidonie. I knew you could be if you made the effort. I'll talk to you tomorrow. Be sure to ring me!" she said, hurrying back to the living room to retrieve gorgeous Jacob. The two of them exiting, leaving behind the mingled aromas of Chanel Number Five (which smelled better on Aunt Claudia than any other woman alive) and Canoe.

I'm beautiful. Six. Size six. God, I *wish* somebody loved me.

Walter Cronkite looked very sober, saddened. Sidonie sat in all her newly acquired magnificence, her throat hurting, watching the seven o'clock news.

"We haven't made the network news, Frank," she said out loud. "They haven't heard about us yet." She laughed, a rather husky, somewhat embittered sound, and got up to prepare her skinny dinner.

She was so apprehensive about the next day, about seeing Frank again she couldn't get to sleep that night. It was amazing to think she could literally dread the sight of someone she'd lived with for eight years. It was all very well to have Aunt Claudia and the hairdresser and makeup lady rhapsodize over her attributes. But inside, she still felt as she had for too long: unnoticed, unnoticeable, unworthy of notice. Fat, drab and dull.

The mirror, with its contradicting image, seemed like some sort of delusionary trick—something hung on the wall to convince her of things not true. In order to remain aware of her new dimensions, her new "look," she ran her fingertips again and again down the sides of her ribcage, over her hipbones. Fingertips conveying reality. I'm in better condition, better shape than I've ever been. So why do I still feel fat? Why do I feel so ugly?

No man in his right mind would want me without the flashy clothes, the cleverly disheveled hair and brilliant makeup. Because, underneath, I'm still the same dumpy cook-and-cleaning-lady I've been all these years. And the first time any man gets close enough to look, he's going to see, know what I really am. How do you stop—if you've been programmed, as Aunt Claudia insists I've been—the program?

Species of North American female known as the suburban housewife. I never really stopped to think about that, or was aware of the category. Not really aware inside my skull. Always refusing to acknowledge that the term applied to me. It was for all those others who didn't know their status. So how could I mind? You have to be looking to see the evolutionary process taking place, to witness the shrinking of self, the loss of identity. If you're not looking, if you haven't the self-awareness or the interest to be looking, it just sneaks up on you, and happens while you're peeling the potatoes, stuffing the pork chops and soaking the green beans.

Why should I be scared of seeing you, Frank, after three months? God, Frank, you're so small! And I thought you were *the one*. Because you had those mysterious attributes that come a set to a male customer. Jesus, Frank! Every guy in the world—barring victims of bizarre accidents and birth defects—has a set. But I was so in awe of yours, I could scarcely get myself through the fussy rituals, I was so busy planning our big moment. All the way through the ceremony, thinking of the two of us finally alone, getting down to it. Going through that whole mumbo-jumbo. Do you? Do *you?* thinking the whole time of getting out of my clothes and under you.

And what did you do? You got so stinking drunk you could hardly stand up, passed out right in the middle of counting up the wedding-gift money we'd received. Slept the whole damned night in your tux, then staggered into the bathroom the next morning to vomit so hideously that I retched in sympathetic response and hid my head under the pillow trying not to hear you. Then came out of the bathroom in all your hairy splendor with an erection out to there, full of passion at eight-forty in the morning, even your skin reeking of Scotch. Cursory attention given to mouth-kisses, a couple of disinterested hand-passes over the victim's still-warm body and then the commencement of the battle: your body against mine, your determination to batter open the door to my closely hoarded virginity. Like some huge snub-nosed bullet repeatedly fired until the target is destroyed. Pushing and pushing. Red-faced 'and distant, embarked on this independent effort. Until your face twisted agonizingly and all your foul, pent-up morning breath exploded in my face with a loud cry as you fell on me like a sack of wet cement. Before pulling yourself out, like a cork from a too-tight bottle (nothing *ever* hurt that much) and rolling away to fall asleep. I walked around with a look on my face people interpreted as the rosy glow of bridal satisfaction. The rosy glow due entirely to having been subjected to the abrading pleasure of your preshave morning face and the dubious honor of becoming a living envelope for your special delivery messages, complete with glue.

Scared of you? I hate you. I hate *me* for staying after that first morning when every bone in my body, every fiber of my being was telling me to get packed and go home. But how could I? My mother would've turned me around and sent me back to you. Daddy, though. He'd have sent me to Tasmania to research the aborigines. Anything to prevent me from continuing what he thought was an outrageous mistake from the word go. ("Stop pushing her, Elizabeth! Half the reason she's considering marrying that lamebrain is because you insist on treating him like royalty.")

I didn't want to hear the arguments you two had, didn't want to listen. Daddy, I wish you were here. I wish we could talk. I've only really known two men in my life, you know. You and Frank. And I *loved* you. Had to go and die at your office one morning. Explosions in your brain they called multiple strokes. My best friend. The only man I've ever known I could talk to. Gone. Not here anymore. Leaving me Frank. And mother. Who, incredibly, began to slowly wilt and fade after you died.

You really loved dad, didn't you, mother? I never believed, until then, that you did. Lost all your liberalism, your drive for "causes," and willed yourself to die because living alone was more than you could bear without daddy to disagree with, without daddy to tease and appease and cajole and love. Dying intestate so that three years later the estate is still tied up in probate and it may take forever before I receive what's rightfully mine. Why the hell couldn't you have written a will? Didn't you love me? If you'd loved me, you'd have protected me. And I'd have a house of my own to live in right now and the security, at least, of some money in the bank. But you were so lost in your swamp of grief you made no provisions for me. Always insisting you loved me so much. Then going ahead, dying, leaving me planted in the suburbs with Frank who had no skills with growing things.

What a funny woman you were. If I was dirty or untidy, no hugs, no kisses. Hugs and kisses are for clean, pretty little girls. Don't, darling! You'll soil mummy's dress. Run along to your room and tidy up, darling. Then come see mummy.

By the time I'd washed my hands and tidied up, I didn't feel like hugging and kissing you. I was mad at you by then. Daddy was never that way. He'd throw me around, ride me on his knee; laughing, tickling me. Until you'd happen by to look disapproving, saying, "Lucas, you'll overexcite her!" Didn't you know children need that kind of over excitement, you stupid woman? It's called demonstration of love. I couldn't get enough in that house. And you pushed and pushed at me, shoving me toward someone I was led to believe could simply me with all I needed. I should have known if you picked him, he'd measure up to your tidy, nice-neat standards. Didn't you notice his white socks? Or did you only notice that they were clean? I'll bet you pretended all kinds of things. How could I let you organize my life that way? I remember Leslie Browning saying one time, "Don't you ever do anything because *you* want to do it? I mean, not that I don't think your mom's really nice and all that. But I mean, she's so pushy, sort of. Not pushy like—I don't know. I just think you sort of do everything she tells you without fighting back. You don't fight for your rights."

Tell you the truth, Leslie, I didn't know I *had*

any. No one bothered to inform me. Daddy tried sometimes. But I was so busy being mummy's good little girl there wasn't any room inside my head for the dangerous act of demanding *rights*. I didn't even know—to show you how ignorant I was— I had the right to get angry with *you* for criticizing my mother.

My mother. You didn't tell me anything I needed to know. None of it. Sex education. One session in Grade Ten. Miss Goodwin. Prematurely gray phys-ed teacher with the pretty face, looking so flummoxed by the questions the kids asked. That idiot Gale what's-her-name talking about standing on her head when she was having a period. Miss Goodwin's face turning scarlet. But she answered the idiotic question. Everybody hated Gail. Me, I had several hundred questions but I couldn't get my hand up. Not even when she asked, "Any questions?" What I wanted to ask, I wanted to ask you how it felt having a man put himself inside of you. But I knew you'd have a coronary. And I wouldn't make myself look too great, either. So, no questions. With evident relief, pretty gray-haired Miss Goodwin went on to the intimacies of touch football. And I went home knowing no more than I had.

God, I don't even know if I like sex, making love. That's so pathetic. Twenty-nine and I don't know if I like it, if I have any aptitude for it. Picking up helpful suggestions from men's magazines and novels, trying to get clues from people who write about these things. But nobody ever actually comes right out and tells you the for-real sensations, what it's all about. Advice columns. Some hired hack dreaming up questions and answers, writing fake letters; probably living in a state of withdrawal, either disgusted by the job or by sex or both. My girlfriend doesn't like . . . My boyfriend says . . . Couples photographed for *Penthouse*, marathon sessions of two people joined in so many impossible positions, looking as if they're having a sensational time—faking or not faking. Looking so absolutely gorgeous—perfect bodies, perfect fit every time. When I certainly never looked or felt remotely gorgeous with Frank-the-Jackhammer digging up my roadbed. So romantic. Can't you for chrissake lift your legs? It hurts, Frank. *You* wouldn't know. Nobody ever asked you to enjoy yourself with your knees jammed back to your shoulders. It's simply impossible to forget yourself when you're being forced to perform like an acrobat for someone else's pleasure. Not your own. What did you ever do for me? Not one damned thing. Nothing. Niente. Zero. *Nothing.* If that part of it had been good I might never have considered leaving. But no. Turn the woman into a human pretzel and cram yourself into the available orifice convinced your very presence in there has to be the essence of every earthly delight. A moron, Frank. A certifiable cretin. Insensitive, white-socked, hard-cocked bastard! If I never do anything else, I'm going to show up tomorrow looking so good, so self-possessed and in control you'll have to take notice, be forced to see you couldn't defeat or one-up me. Every guy's got one, Frank. But you think yours makes you extraordinary. And you're not, never were. I'd rather do without than do with you.

Well, not without. Without *you*. But not without altogether. Because now that there's no one, I sometimes feel as if I'm going to go completely crazy or die from living untouched. How do people live alone and like it? How do they learn, adjust? I don't like it. I feel so separated, cut off from everything I knew. But I didn't like what I knew. It's so hard making changes.

Maybe I'd feel the same way about any man. Being expected to perform first thing in the morning with a full bladder and a bad taste in the mouth. No chance to prepare. I don't know. But I'd like a chance to find out, to know if I respond or not, if I like it or not. A chance to know. Something more than I've had.

FOUR

She managed to keep a calm exterior throughout the brief proceedings, smiling into Frank's
confounded face. He kept looking at her with an
expression of shocked bewilderment as if the wrong
woman—or a stark-naked one—had mistakenly
arrived to witness the dissolution of somebody else's
marriage. At last, the pronouncement that what
had once been was no more and all were free to go
their merry ways.

She was so depressed she went straight to the
nearest decent-looking bar, sat down on a stool in
the rosy gloom and began drinking ryes-and-ginger
with suicidal absorption. Too brought down to go
anywhere or call anyone. Poking a stir-stick up
and down, up and down while the ice diluted the
taste of the drink. She didn't really want to get
drunk but what the hell else was there to do? And
guys were always going out getting drunk when the
news was bad or Black Bart was in town. So why
not?

She sat brooding, staring into the depths of her glass, absent-mindedly blotting up drops of condensation that formed on the highly polished bar. With cocktail napkins. A pile of them so handily nearby. Trying to think of where to take her denuded life. What to do with it. My life. Heavy as lead, the prospect of this emptied life; this prospectless life of emptiness.

Frank saying, "What *happened* to you? I wouldn't have *recognized* you." An expression on his face. One of those telling looks that, translated, meant he'd have liked doing some pretzel-bending. Just for old time's sake. Never mind that he'd brought his girlfriend along. For company? Moral support?

She'd turned at the end to see Frank meeting up with a sickly blonde in the corridor outside. A tiny, stick-doll blonde with bland, waxy features and adoring hands, looking rapturously up into Frank's handsome Ken-doll face. Baby Chrissie and her very own Ken-doll. There really was another woman. Or else he brought one along just for the occasion.

I don't even like you. I shouldn't care. I shouldn't. So why do I feel so stripped, so deprived? I did the dumping, had the upper hand for a change. But it doesn't feel that way. Marching off down the corridor of the courthouse with Baby Chrissie's head cuddling against his all-protecting shoulder. You had to make one last point, Frank; had to make quite sure the blade was in right to the hilt. I don't like you. Don't like your tactics, never did. So why do I feel so bad?

At a small table in the corner, Michael Quinn was trying to get Beau Bannon, self-acclaimed superstud and star of a handful of hugely money-making skin flicks, to concentrate for just a few minutes on the business at hand.

Mike, who'd originally entered into film production with lofty ideas of creating a more liberal art form (or at least contributing to a noteworthy degree) had, after discovering the world was filled with high-minded artistic film producers, turned from his idealistic goals toward making money. And his films made more money than he knew what to do with. Underground films with underground people, Beau Bannon his most popular male performer, making several fortunes in dollars, leaving Mike with a permanent malaise and still-lingering ideas of doing something more with his talent and money than producing a lot of storyless, tasteless, badly photographed movies of two or more semi-attractive people fake-fucking. Or for-real fucking, depending upon the mood of said semiattractive participants.

Beau Bannon (née Arthur Jacobson) believed himself to be the in-person purveyor of sex-at-its-best and went about proving it to any number of willing women he encountered as a direct result of his enjoyable efforts in Mike's films. At twenty-six, he was convinced he could move up from the shabby but lucrative realm of porno-flicks to the golden-hued environs of honest-to-God movies; seeing himself as the ultimate replacement for Robert Redford. Aside from possessing a neatly circumcised appendage of beyond-average proportions, he was, he would humbly concede, a great-looking guy. And he didn't mind hearing how great as often as it could be introduced into any conversation.

Michael Jamieson Quinn, not unaware of certain of the baser realities of life while indulging Beau's vanity, was completely aware of the marketability of this brainless stud's attributes. Beau was capable of getting it up blindfolded in a blizzard. And that was money at the box office. Beau also had a mouthful of very, very expensive caps that gave him a spectacular smile. Although audiences, Mike had long since noted, rarely looked above Beau's navel.

Michael Jamieson Quinn, age thirty-eight, pornoflick millionaire and dissatisfied artist, spent his off-camera time with Beau inwardly heaving exasperated sighs. Trying to cope with Beau's boring vanity and yet get on with the details of the next project was almost more than Mike could stand.

So now, for the third time, he tried to get Beau's attention turned toward their next film. But Beau was so intrigued, so wildly turned on by the redhead at the bar he wasn't listening to a thing Mike was saying.

"Look at that!" he said to Mike. "Is that something? D'you ever in your life see such a dynamite piece? That is righteous tail, man!"

"Man," Mike said tiredly (at once realizing Beau would interpret the remark favorably), "you're something else yourself." God, what a pain in the ass trying to talk to Beau. An investment was an investment. But one of these days, he'd have to find somebody less arrogant, less vain, less boring, less everything to replace Beau. The fact was, Mike couldn't stand him. "Look," Mike persisted, "could we get this settled?"

"Feature that in skin, man!" Beau said excitedly, rising like a cobra to the music. "Tell you what," he said eagerly. "You need a new chick, right? A thousand in my pocket free and clear says I can get you that one."

"Will you cool it," Mike said patiently. "Could you for maybe ten seconds pay some attention?"

"Make it better," Beau said, "I'll *bet* you a thousand. She does it, you pay me. She doesn't, I pay you. But a thousand cash says I can get that chick to do the flick with me."

Mike, surprised by this rare display of gambling spirit, looked up for the first time, directing his eyes to the bar. To see what in hell this idiot was babbling about. And seeing the woman at the bar was like having his lungs suddenly punctured so that they collapsed, leaving him insufficient air to breathe; a humming in his ears and a manic thumping in his chest. He drew in his breath very slowly, angling for a better view. Beautiful. But obviously on a downer, running long fingers up and down the length of her glass, staring fixedly at the bar. She looked like the perfect one, the one he'd been looking for forever. She was the one he'd always needed for His Movie. Desperate to know if she looked as good up close, if she sounded good, he said to Beau, "You're on! I'll take the bet."

At once, having said this, Mike felt awful. What

kind of ridiculous bullshit was this, making a bet
on a woman? That's how Beau treats people. Not
me. A cruddy thing to do, making a bet on a chick
as if she were a racehorse or something. But having
agreed to it, there was no way he could—all in the
same minute—back off. Because he had to hear
her voice, hear how she'd sound and what she'd
have to say, see her face up close and check out
her smile.

Beau flung his hand across the table. "We'll
shake on it," he said, then pushed back his chair.

"What're you doing?" Mike wanted to know, a
little alarmed at how quickly this was getting out of
hand. I don't need any of this. With this pea-brain
calling the shots.

"Can't get to her if we don't talk. Come on. Just
let me play it. Be cool."

Sidonie was thinking she ought to go home. Call
Aunt Claudia, let her know how it had gone. It
had indeed gone. Over. Unmarried again. With
three hundred of Frank's dollars monthly until such
time as she remarried. Which was just funny. Re-
marry who? The rottenest, lowest feeling, probably
the darkest, meanest mood she'd ever been in. Like
quicksand sucking her down into something thick
and permanent. If only there was something I could
do, something I knew how to do. Something.

She was aware of people sliding onto the stools on
either side of her but didn't look up, trying to
pursue an elusive thought. It had to do with working,
finding some sort of legitimate employment. Because if she had to spend every day and night in

the apartment exercising, trying to stay away from the refrigerator, she'd go straight out of her mind. In a month, she'd be fat again. And very suicidal. *I have to do something.*

"Hi!" Beau said, flashing his best smile like a press pass.

She didn't look up, unaware he was addressing her.

"Hi!" Beau tried again, tapping on the bar to get the bartender's attention. "Give the lady a refill," Beau said munificently, dropping a twenty on the bar.

Sidonie turned—in the direction away from the voice—to see a black-haired, blue-eyed, big-featured man looking somewhat embarrassed, smiling apologetically.

"Beau's trying to buy you a drink," Mike said.

She looked blankly at him for several seconds, then turned to have a look at this Beau person. A kid with bleached hair and empty-looking eyes.

"What?" She looked at Mike once more. "Sorry?"

"Could we buy you a drink?" Mike offered, crazy about the sound of her voice. But not so crazy about the shell-shocked look to her eyes.

"Oh!" Sidonie smiled. "Thank you." She turned to smile at the kid, then back again to the man. Very adult-looking, all grown up. "Am I being picked up?" she asked, looking into the blue eyes, wondering if this adult-looking man went around picking up women in bars for a hobby. He wouldn't have too many problems. So what? She felt herself being slowly lifted out of the muck of her mood. And that was fine.

Mike laughed. She had a smile as good as the voice. He couldn't believe it.

"Beau's tackling the pick-up angle," he said truthfully. "I just think you're beautiful. So if you don't mind, I'll sit here and look at you for however long it takes me to drink my drink and then we'll run along."

"Beautiful?" She laughed. "You're going to sit there and look at me? You're crazy!"

"I'm not too well." He grinned.

Beau was getting annoyed, receiving no attention. He touched her on the arm as the bartender set down her drink. "Here y'go!" Beau said, letting loose another of his best smiles as he held out his hand. "Beau Bannon. That's Mike Quinn."

Sidonie reluctantly shook his hand, finding the situation hilarious as she swiveled to offer her hand to the one called Mike.

"My name's Sidonie. I'm celebrating my divorce."

"Sidney?" Mike asked.

"Sid-o-nie. French. But I'm not French. Just the name." Mike took hold of her hand and the most amazing thing happened inside her. Everything in her shouted, "HELLO!" Shocking her.

"Fun, isn't it?" Mike commiserated. "I did that number once. Leaves you feeling like garbage afterward. As if a whole hunk of your life just got wiped clean like a blackboard and you're right back where you started. Except a lot older and tireder."

"That's right," she said softly, slowly withdrawing her hand. "That's exactly how it feels. How long were you married?"

"Three years. You?"

"Eight."

"Eight? Married at twelve, right?"

"Not quite. But thank you."

"Sidonie," he said, savoring the name as he tasted his drink. "What do you do, Sidonie?"

"Do? I don't *do* anything. What do you do?"

"Produce films," he said, gearing himself up for the stock response. The one that came with widened eyes and, Oh is that right? followed by a not-so-subtle outpushing of breasts, insucking of stomach and thrusting-back of shoulders. It sickened him, that stock response.

"What kind of films?" she asked interestedly, leaning on her elbow on the bar. "I love movies."

"Erotic films," Beau answered importantly, power coursing through his body.

"Erotic films?" she asked Mike. "*Erotic* films?"

"That's right." He looked down at his hands, wishing he hadn't given up smoking. He wanted a cigarette so badly he could've screamed.

"You produce erotic films," she repeated, trying to absorb that. "And you," she looked around at Beau, "are a star of these erotic films. Right?"

"Bet your sweet kazoo, babe. Already made seven."

"Well, isn't that wonderful for you?" she said pleasantly, thinking he was a jerk, a real jerk.

Mike, picking up on the note of sarcasm, watched her with increasing interest. You're good, he thought.

You're very, very good. He laughed suddenly, saying, "Sidonie, how about dinner? I'm enjoying you."

She glanced at her watch, noting it was after six, thinking, What the hell? There are only three or four things that can happen. We can have dinner and that'll be that. Or I can wind up in some kind of scene with one or both of them. Which wouldn't be so hot because the jerk makes me nervous. Or they could murder me and dump my body somewhere.

"All right." She smiled at Mike. "Why not?"

"Dynamite!" Beau chuckled, congratulating himself. This was going to be the easiest, fastest thou he'd ever made. Mike shot him a "Cool it!" look which Beau ignored.

Throughout dinner, Beau kept trying to crash the conversation, making non sequiturs, dropping inane remarks about his career, about this and that.

Mike, meanwhile, enormously intrigued by her, questioned Sidonie about her marriage, her life, her views. She volunteered very little real information, providing only a general rundown on suburban married life and her present preoccupation with fixing up her new apartment and worrying over finding a job. Despite the fact that she looked and sounded reasonably all right, he guessed she was suffering through the "crazies" (as he'd called them when he'd had them) brought about by the divorce. But, aside from this, he felt more strongly with each passing minute that he'd finally stumbled across the one woman perfect in every way to play "Honey."

He'd been fantasizing about "Honey," plotting

and planning every detail and nuance of this film he'd one day make for close to ten years. Wherever he went, whatever he did, he was always looking for the right woman. And now—he couldn't believe his luck!—he'd found her. But finding her and actually getting the film going were two things separated by any number of logistical problems. Problems or no, though, he was crazy about this Sidonie; liked everything about her, right down to her ankles.

Every time she looked at Michael's mouth, she felt that familiar aching in her groin. All the while they were talking, all she could think was, I should go home. If I don't, I'm going to be in some kind of trouble. But I don't want to go home. Home was empty, lonely, a nice place where one woman had already died. She felt her mind sliding toward consideration of that lovely, long-dead woman and pulled herself back sharply. To look at Michael's mouth again. He seemed like a nice man. Especially compared to the kid, who really was coming on like gangbusters, doing everything but flexing his pec's.

Mike. Michael Quinn. You're so good looking. If this is a routine, it's a very, very good one. I think it is. I can't tell. I wish I knew more. I wish I knew how to be blasé and in control. Sophisticated. But I don't. I can't tell if you're for real or just some kind of con-artist. I *can* tell you think this kid Beau is a jerk and I agree with you. You produce porno movies and you know what? I've always wanted to see one. Never have.

"I've never seen one of those movies," she told Mike. "I must be some sort of living anachronism or whatever you call someone who's about thirty years misplaced. Frank went all the time. I'd read about some movie and Frank would casually say, 'I saw that. It wasn't much.' But he never did take me to see one."

"You haven't missed much," Mike said, meaning it. "What I've always wanted to do is make a good movie, something involving. But people who can act, people with any kind of real talent don't come knocking at my door asking to do my flicks at two bills a day."

"Two hundred dollars a day?"

"That's the going rate."

"How long does it usually take to make one of your movies?"

"Five, six shooting days."

"That's an awful lot of money."

"Depends on **how** you look at it," he said, praying she wasn't going to express an interest in making herself some money. If she was one of those, "Honey" was blown before it ever got off the ground. "What we put out in five or six days' shooting isn't exactly art."

"I suppose not," she said, trying to imagine some, any, or all of it; her imagination failing due to insufficient fodder.

"Never seen one, eh?" Beau asked.

"No, never."

"Hey, Mike! Let's show her one! What d'ya say? Let's split to my pad and show Sidney a flick."

"Sidonie," she corrected, watching Mike.

"Sidonie, excuse us for a minute," Mike said, getting up from the table. "Beau and I have a little something we have to talk about."

Beau didn't budge, failing to get the drift.

"Beau?" Mike said quietly. "You mind?"

She watched the two men go, thinking, I'm not even drunk. So whatever happens, I've got no excuses, nobody to blame. Except myself for possible stupidity and enormous curiosity. She knew Michael was going to get rid of the jerk. And she was glad. Because Beau was a little too reminiscent of Frank. A rammer, a crammer, a damage-doer. Whatever happened with Michael, she felt quite sure he wasn't the heedless, proceed-regardless type. She had the arbitrary, perhaps even irrational idea that he was the kind of man who'd stop whatever he was doing if asked.

Mike stood inside the men's room waiting for Beau to enter. And the instant he did, Mike said, "Split, Beau! That's *it* for tonight!"

"How d'you figure that, eh?" Beau got very red in the face.

"I figure it. That's all."

"It was *my* idea, man!"

"The woman doesn't *like* you, man. And she's definitely out of the question for your next flick. So forget it!"

"You're outa your fucking gourd!" Beau declared. "She likes me just as much as she likes you. What's with the big scene, anyway? She's just out to score.

83

Or maybe you're just trying to renege on our bet."

"Forget it! Just split, okay? You've had yourself a nice, free steak. Now run along home like a good boy. Call up one of your girlfriends or something. But split! Now!"

"You use her and you don't pay me, I'll be around to collect. You dig?"

"Good night, Artie." Mike smiled.

Beau was outraged. "Don't you fuck with me, Quinn! You . . . I . . ." Words wouldn't come. He wrenched open the men's room door, turned to glare at Mike for a count of three, then stalked off.

Mike took a deep breath, then walked over to the urinal. Might as well, since he was already in there. And while he was at it, he might as well call and cancel Grace.

Sidonie nursed her coffee, lit a cigarette. It was taking quite a while. Maybe the jerk didn't want to go. It didn't matter how long it took. I'm not going anywhere. I've got all night. Forever, for that matter. What's there to hurry for?

About the only thing I'm good for is cooking. Insulting bastard, Frank. I wonder how it would be to have a restaurant, do all the cooking. Probably get fat, sampling all the food. But maybe not. All that rushing around, having a business, that would keep it off.

She visualized a homey sort of place. With a fireplace. And maybe a couple of sofas, coffee tables instead of the usual bar where people would wait for their tables. Like a living room or an old-fashioned inn instead of the typical business. Like this place, she thought. This is so typical. I'd have trestle tables instead of standard commercial-type tables. No tablecloths. Mats of some kind. With mismatched serving pieces. Like someone's home. No ketchup bottles on the table. Salt and pepper mills. Comfortable chairs to sit in. Nice, clean floorboards. Waitresses in long dresses with pinafore-type aprons. Hurricane lamps. A limited menu, only four or five main courses. That's all. No printed menus. One salad. One dressing. One dessert.

She could see it. A quiet, relaxed place with first-class food and service. No loud drunks at the bar. No red-jacketed bartender. A woman to mix drinks. Women in the kitchen.

Grace put down the telephone and kicked off her shoes. He does it every time, she thought, heading for the bedroom to remove her finery. Every single time. Something came up, Grace. I'll tell you what it was, Mike. It's between your legs and comes up like the dawn. In her dressing gown, she went to the bar to pour herself a drink, then picked up the *TV Guide* to see if there was anything on worth seeing. Nothing. Reruns and game shows. Merv Griffin.

It's about your grand illusions, Mike. Those and your utter inability to consider, ever, who you're affecting and how with these things you do. She lifted her glass thinking, Good luck out there, whoever you are.

"Sorry to be so long," Mike apologized. "I couldn't stand another minute of him."

"I couldn't either." She smiled. "I'm glad you did that."

"More coffee?"

"I'd love some." She felt easier now, more ready to relax as she sat back and he ordered fresh cups of coffee.

"Do you like what you do?" she asked him.

"Like it? Some, I guess. It isn't what I started out to do, you know. I mean, I don't think anybody sets out *planning* to make a career out of skin flicks."

"Oh?"

"Mind if I borrow that?" He indicated her cigarette.

"Not at all." She gave it to him, watched as he took a deep drag. "Would you like a cigarette? I have lots."

"I've given them up," he answered, looking as if he'd rarely enjoyed anything quite so much as the taste of her cigarette. "I need a taste every so often."

"When did you give them up?"

"A couple of weeks ago. It's murder. Anyway, where were we?"

"What you started out to do," she prompted.

"Oh, right! I was into making *good* movies." He smiled and shook his head. "Every other dude around was out to do the same gig. So I made a pile of bread instead."

"Your movies make a lot of money?"

"I'm no moralist, you know, Sidonie. I mean, how can I be? But I know what I'm doing. I mean, there are a hell of a lot of people go to see a skin flick, dig it for what it is. Right? It's a kick, a turn-on, no big complicated number. But there are a lot who can't handle it. I mean, not everybody's all that out front with sex. Go to see a skin flick and bombs go off in their heads. Don't know what to do with it, how to handle it. I can see that, see how dangerous it might be for some people. And that's the part that really brings me down."

"Go on. Tell me why."

"Look, let's put it this way: I'm pretty typical. Okay?"

"If you say so." She couldn't resist smiling. If he was typical she'd just won the Garbo look-alike award for '75.

"Well, okay." He smiled back. "For the sake of argument, I'm pretty typical."

"All right."

"Right. So, I'm pretty typical. I was taught all the no-no's and the dark-sided stuff about who and how and where and when and what. But we all get to grow up a little somewhere along the line. Anyway, what I'm saying is, I can see a skin flick and get what I want out of it. It's not going to blow my brain and give me a whole bunch of wild ideas so I go out and start putting it to girls, raping, beating. You follow me?"

She nodded.

"Right. But a lot of guys, seeing it all up there, raw, right in their faces, it's too much. They can't handle that much all in one shot. Their heads aren't in the right places. Whatever. Like these cats reading hard porn. It does something to them. Brings out all kinds of hostility, anger. Whatever. But it brings it all out. So, what I'm saying is, I can't just get these flicks out there and then pretend I don't know every so often there's a dude watching who's going to get freaked totally out of shape because of what he's seeing in one of my flicks. Because, if you want to get right down to it, if that guy goes out and does a heavy number on some woman, it's a little bit my fault for helping push him over the edge."

"If you feel that way, why don't you stop?"

"I don't know why," he said truthfully. "I think about it. A lot. But there's nothing else I like doing. Movies are my thing. And one of these days I'm going to get it on with a really decent, really right up there flick."

"Are they that bad?"

"It depends, Sidonie. It depends, as I said, on where your head's at."

"I would like to see one. It's hard to discuss moral issues when I don't know what I'm talking about."

"Are you saying you'd like me to show you one?"

She hadn't expected so direct a response.

"You'd show me one?" she asked, thinking it was like coming straight out and saying, "I'm available for practically anything."

"Look, I don't want you to get the wrong impression. I mean, I'm not into this thing where I invite women up to my place to show them movies. My place is where I live. I know it's corny but there's something to it. I don't mean I wouldn't like to invite you back. I mean I just don't have a big routine like that. You know? Where I say, 'How about coming back, we'll eyeball a flick and get it on a little?' That's not my bag. I want you to know that out front. If you'd like to come, see one, I'll show you a movie. But any time you've had enough and you're ready to go, let me know and I'll take you home. Okay?"

I've actually asked him to take me home with him. He must think I'm awfully eager. Or something.

"Okay," she agreed.

He must like me. He really must. You don't just take someone to your apartment unless you like them, unless you feel something—the beginning of something—for them. Somebody likes me.

She felt unreasonably happy. And bursting with anticipation. God! The things that could happen.

FIVE

He paid the tab and they went outside to be faced with the problem of two cars.

"You can follow me in your car," he said, disappointed he wasn't going to have her company on the drive. He'd been looking forward to the cozy intimacy provided by the close interior of a car. It always gave him a good feeling, driving along with a pretty woman beside him.

Feeling slightly chilled, she went to her old station wagon and got in, hands shaky as she pushed in the ignition key, her knees bouncing around uncontrollably as she backed out of her slot and began following him through the streets. She was very tempted to keep on going, drive home. He didn't know where she lived or very much about her. He'd probably never be able to find her.

When she saw where he was headed, she thought for one crazy moment that he'd somehow managed to find out after all where she lived. But he kept on going. On to the opposite side of the Park.

"You won't believe it," she told him, meeting up with him in front of his building. "I live about three blocks from here. On the other side of the Park."

"No kidding! I'm big on this part of town. Come on up."

It was a large, rambling apartment, surprisingly furnished in magnificent antiques.

"This is beautiful," she said, admiring the Victorian sofa, newly upholstered in deep burgundy velvet. "You have some wonderful pieces."

"I'll run it down here," he said, leading the way along the corridor to a room outfitted like a small theater. "I'm more into movies than anything else." He switched on the light and began sorting through round, gray metal containers. "Ever since I was a kid, movies have really turned me on. It's a trip having my own screening room."

There were three modern, unfussy sofas in dark gray. A scattering of small smoked-glass tables with ashtrays.

He watched her looking around. "Sit down," he said, winding the film on the projector. "Relax. This one's about the best of the bag. Featuring our modest young horse, Beau."

"If you dislike him, why do you work with him?" she asked, settling herself on the center sofa, sinking deep into the soft cushions.

"He's good at what he does. Which isn't saying a whole hell of a lot. Who knows? We all get tied up in things and then don't know, later on, how to get out. Anyway, here goes!"

He hit the lights, adjusted the focus, then went

to sit down beside her on the sofa saying, "Just give me the word and it goes off."

"All right," she said, her eyes on the screen. There was an unreal feeling about this. She couldn't manage to make herself unaware that she was alone with this man in his apartment. It was, in fact, the first grown man's apartment she'd ever been in. Discounting Frank's room at the dorm. Which was hardly an apartment. Had she ever thought about it, which she hadn't, she wouldn't have expected a man to display such fine taste in furnishings, to be surrounded by so many well-cared-for and highly polished pieces she herself might have liked living with.

Mike kept his eyes moving back and forth between her and the screen. He'd been wondering up until that moment if she'd been telling the truth. But witnessing her initial reaction, he knew there was no way on earth she'd ever seen a skin flick before. Her eyes got wider and wider, her hand went to her mouth as a disbelieving smile took form. He watched her eyes closely, saw her mouth open slightly.

Sidonie couldn't believe what she was seeing. I don't *believe* this! She smiled involuntarily seeing the two people on the screen throwing off their clothes within minutes of meeting in a laundromat, having exchanged some unintelligible words of silly-sounding dialogue accompanied by witless smiles and supposedly meaningful badinage. Stereotypical image of a schoolteacher with bun and glasses. Removing the glasses (with a leer), unpinning her hair to become the beauty (???) we all knew was there all the time under the too-long shapeless skirt and drab sweater. And Beau, for God's sake! She'd never have believed a man could be constructed that way. He didn't look human. She watched, riveted, feeling herself beginning to perspire as the two up there started doing things she'd not only never dreamed she might see in a movie but things she'd never dreamed of doing. It certainly wasn't beautiful. Exciting. God! But grotesque. When the camera zoomed between the girl's legs, Sidonie thought her eyes would fall right out of her head. She could feel them bulging against the front of her face. That's gross! Absolutely gross! How could she *do* it? Forgetting herself, she held the hand Mike offered, beginning to feel very strange, wanton. Watching Beau's tongue exaggeratedly flicking between the girl's wide-spread legs. Ugly. But fascinating. Horrible seeing a woman like that, in that way. Terrible. Awful. Yet excitement was building inside her like a fever. Heat spreading up, down, fanning outward.

Mike held her hand, running his thumb back and forth over her knuckles, knowing what was going to happen. And feeling a little guilty. Because she'd never seen anything like this before and it was taking advantage in a big way. Which he hated. But I want you. And I need to know if you're all the way right.

Innocent. She seemed so innocent it was hard to believe she was as old as she'd said she was. Her reactions showing so plainly on her face. Like a

kid's. So visual. The perfect face. But she's no baby.
She knows what she's doing. And Beau was right
about one thing. She's put together like dynamite.

She became aware of him. Slowly. Feeling his
hand tighten around hers. Rock music soundtrack
and garbled voices, sounds. This blue-eyed man
looking at me with a look I know. I know that look.
I want it I don't care it's one time out of my whole
life and I don't have anything else, not one thing.
It's not the worst thing that could ever happen to
me. It isn't as if I'm being filmed and I think you're
so good-looking. If you hadn't come along, I'd be
sitting home alone now feeling so bad, hating being
alone more than I've ever hated anything. The way
you look at me. As if you really think I'm beautiful.
I'm going to I'll never see you again so what does
it matter. It doesn't matter. Just, please, don't be
another Frank. I can't take any more disappointments.

In a darkened room with technicolored bodies
horribly exposed like willing victims to some newly
devised form of torture that lasts for hours. She
leaned fractionally closer and Mike gathered her
into his arms, delighted as always by the frailty
of the female body, the fragility of small bones
beneath the surface and the giddying crush of
rounded breasts against his chest. He kissed that
wide red mouth, instantly lost to the pounding
pleasure of holding all that softness and the warm
eagerness of her mouth. She pulled away breathlessly, looking into his eyes, thinking, Nobody's
ever held me like this, kissed me this way as if he

meant it, holding me as if I was made of glass and might break. She closed her eyes and went back, opening her mouth for more. Nervous, wondering where and how and if he'd undress her or if she'd have to do it herself. Do I wait for him to start touching me or do I start? How to let him know? I don't know what to do.

God! You beautiful thing! He kissed her harder, drawing her closer, drinking in her scent, her sweetness. Loving the way she was growing warmer, the air between them heavy.

Sounds from onscreen; short, sharp cries that reached her ears from a great distance. Color flashes on the walls. Oh my God I'm so excited. Her arms tightening around Mike who was kissing her more forcefully, teeth colliding, tongues dancing an elaborate minuet. Yet his hands remained so gentle on her back, moving languidly. She wanted expected hoped his hands would move, explore. You can touch me. Touch me. All of her attention directed toward those scarcely-moving hands.

What'm I waiting for? he asked himself. Nothing. Except that he was enjoying her so much, taking time to learn the feel of her mouth, the shape of it, having known from the start how good she'd be. Her breasts pressing against him. He slid his hand around onto her breast and she drew her breath in sharply as her hand curved firmly over the back of his neck, fingertips grazing his ear, playing along the line of his jaw.

It's happening, she thought, aware of his hand leaving her breast, following it down as it settled on her knee, where it stayed for several moments before starting to stroke gently upward. His mouth urging her head back, he lifted his body away to untie her belt and open the dress, placing his hands fingers-spayed over her breasts. Beautiful. Able to contain those soft, soft breasts within the boundaries of his hands. Holding her breasts captive, he whispered, "I swear to God I didn't plan this. It wasn't why we bought you a drink."

"It doesn't matter," she whispered back. "It's all right." It doesn't matter. What does it matter? I'm going to be a *Penthouse* spread for real, just once, so I'll know. I want to *know*.

His hands moving, touching, going so slowly she wanted to tell him to hurry. But couldn't speak. Could hear only the sound of her own breathing, echoing in her ears. The movie going on and on, its sounds its music making the unreality more unreal as he peeled her out of her clothes with such clever hands while the movie sent flashes and flickers of changing colors over them. Make me feel good, she thought, finding herself sprawled on the sofa as he removed the last of her clothes and then stood up, all the while his eyes roving over her, to take off his clothes; emerging like some gigantic improbable Titan all aroused and springing eagerly upward from boxer shorts he kicked aside before lowering himself over her, starting to kiss her again. His body moving slowly against her, hard, trapped between their bellies. All so slow, slow, dizzying. Then he began rearranging both of them saying, "Come up here."

"What?" She didn't understand.

He was beneath her now, and telling her to come up. Up where?

He smiled the strangest, hungriest, wet-mouthed smile she'd ever seen. And she felt suddenly stupid, inept. Not knowing what it was he was asking her to do. "Sit up." His voice soft, hands and arms lifting her. She sat on his hips staring down into his face, despairing of her ignorance. What does he want me to do? What?

He shifted, sliding down under her until she realized in one overheated, blushing moment what it was he intended to do. Is there something I'm supposed to do? she wondered frantically as he arranged himself. She looked down (a mistake) to see his eyes looking back at her as the lower half of his face vanished and his hands came up to cover her breasts. Then he opened his mouth. And her face took fire.

My God, God! Michael. Nobody's ever actually done this to me. Putting your mouth on me.

His tongue (just like the damned movie) flicked against her, then, like a mouth-kiss, drew at her, opening and closing, his tongue traveling down, down then darting upward, slowly, then more quickly, faster and then faster. She grabbed hold of his wrists, straining to stay where she was, yet growing taller, her torso lengthening, head lolling, falling backward as his tongue pushed her toward what was going to be the biggest, most . . . Don't think about it! Don't think!

Her eyes were emptied, unseeing; her mouth

open, a sound escaping. He fondled her breasts, watching her, thinking I have to put this on film, show someone like you responding so totally, so willingly. It's all there. The story, the music. Get a first-rate cameraman. Do it. Baby. Love you. Smell so good, taste so good.

I'm going to come. God. Oh God! I can't think about what, the way we're, how you're doing nobody ever did I'm so excited do you do this to all the women you *God!*

She came, her eyes fluttering closed, a wild cry taking flight from her throat as she pitched into it, jerking, starting, writhing blindly. I don't care what you do what you think of me how many women you I feel good it's so good nothing matters you do like me I know you do are we falling in love . . .

He shifted back up, holding her on his chest; her hair falling, covering both their faces so that he had to hold the hair away with both hands to find her mouth, kiss her while she held on to him whispering, "It's just this time and it doesn't matter. You like me, don't you? Don't think I'm terrible but I've been so lonely and Frank always treated me as if I was a sack of dirty laundry. Just pretend. Pretend. For one time so at least I know. Because I want to know. There's so much I don't know. Pretend."

"Hey!" he murmured, "I'm not pretending."

"Doesn't matter, doesn't matter." She kept saying it, making him feel sad and a little sorry for both of them, wanting her, wanting to be right up to there inside her more, harder than he'd ever wanted anything. To have this beautiful baby, so sweet, think him a nice man, find him likable, not judge or condemn him because of the fucking flicks, because of how he made his money. It was like being ripped open, hearing her telling him to pretend, sharing something so intimate, vulnerable together. He'd never thought about it, how a pretty woman might be lonely. It blew his mind, that she could be lonely. And that from the look and feel of it nobody'd ever bothered to give such a dynamite chick a little head. What a waste!

She felt lulled, peaceful enough to go to sleep. He hadn't made love in the way she'd expected. But so nice to have someone pay a little attention to her pleasure. For a change. No matter if it hadn't been the old familiar business. Better, nicer this way than being bent this way and that, hurt. This didn't hurt. But it felt foolish sitting on him that way. Foolish but fantastic. So she could easily sleep; felt wonderfully sleepy, calmed.

"You okay?" he asked, enjoying the weight of her head on his shoulder, her breath soft on his neck. Mmm! He squeezed her. One delicious, beautiful package of goods.

"I'm fine," she said in a whisper. "Thank you. I've never . . . done that before. Different, but I . . . I liked it."

"Hey!" He laughed, turning so he could see her face. "I could tell you haven't. But that's not all, babe. You think that's the whole trip?"

She blushed again, hating the transparency of

her reactions, her inability to keep things to herself. Always saying whatever was in her mind.

"Baby, that's just for openers!" He laughed again, knocked out by her. What unbelievable luck! To find a chick without big plans for how she wanted to be laid. "Too tired?" he asked.

"I'm not tired."

"How come?" he asked, curious.

"How come what?"

"How come it was your first time?"

"I wasn't any good. I'm sorry."

"Who said you were no good?"

"I . . . it's just that I don't know what . . . who's supposed to do what."

"Baby, nobody's *supposed* to do anything. You just enjoy it, go with it. What the hell were you married to anyway?"

"I don't know. I used to be very fat, you know, Michael. Maybe that's why. I don't know."

"What's fat got to do with it?"

"I'm not sure." Why don't I shut up? "I don't look as good without the makeup. I mean, at home, when it's just me, I look terrible."

"Everybody looks terrible at home." He smiled, really getting such a charge out of her. "And you couldn't be that bad," he went on. "You're beautiful. Better than that."

"Thank you," she croaked, another scorching blush on the rise.

He didn't say anything more but dropped his head and began kissing her again; kissing her ears and throat, her shoulders, her breasts. And while

101

he was kissing her, his hands roamed up and down her arms and legs, across her ribs and belly, down between her thighs. She didn't know what to do for him. She let her hands move experimentally on his chest and down his arms, around over his back, loving the feel of his skin, his warmth, his increasing warmth. When suddenly he pulled his mouth away from hers, moving very quickly, draped her legs over his shoulders and once more pushed his mouth at her.

His choice of positions seemed to trap her into nonresponding with any other part of herself. All she could do was touch the top of his head, his shoulders. And she did. Hesitantly, gratefully, humbly. So moved by his wanting to make her feel good. And she did. Feel good. As if somebody had cut her head off at the neck and turned her into one vast ravenous mouth. She shuddered and gasped. He made her come again. Twice in one night. The best thing that had ever happened to her. But he wasn't stopping. Going on even though she'd finished and needed to stop, rest. The pleasure replaced by a teeth-clenching kind of agony.

"Please." She touched the top of his head. "Stop!"

At once, he lifted his head and climbed back on top of her.

"What's the matter, babe?" he asked, kissing her forehead, playing with her hair.

"I couldn't. I can't keep on going that way. It starts to hurt."

"It happens that way with some chicks," he said knowingly.

"What?"

He touched her throat. "A lot of guys are that way, too. Need a little break in between. Most guys can't just come and then dive back right away for more. Some chicks get sort of swollen inside."

"You must know quite a few women," she said, pierced by this revelation, feeling a little less special because of his knowing disclosures.

"Some. I'm no Beau, though. That guy's plain ridiculous. Fuck anything."

Is that how people talk? she wondered, disliking his expressions.

"You like it on top?" he asked, stroking her between the thighs, making her squirm, checking her face for reactions. What a great chick! No objections. All kinds of staying power.

"You mean the way we did before?"

"No, like you on top, me inside."

She hated it, having to answer his questions like some exotic anatomy lecture.

"Would you like that?" she asked, fighting down her objections.

"Only if it's a turnon for you, babe."

"Sure I would," she lied, not knowing what she would or wouldn't like. I'm getting educated. A crash course in positions.

Back on top of him again. Trying not to think about how she looked, about her nakedness. Naked in an entirely new way. Naked with Frank had always had a certain absent-minded nothingness to it. Primarily because he'd never seemed to be looking, never seemed to notice whether or not she had any clothes on. But this man. He was noticing everything. And commenting on what he noticed. Making her acutely aware of the ridiculous aspects of her being naked with a man one step removed from being a complete stranger; finding herself preparing—with all the diligence of a good student working toward A grades—to take this man inside herself. In a posture she'd never before attempted. In a frame of mind mainly uncertain. But determined to follow as far as he could lead, to find out about herself in the process.

So. Disregarding the flush of heated color hanging from her cheekbones like a climber clinging to a rockface by his fingernails, tenaciously, insistently, unbudging, she began tackling the problem of how to go about placing herself on him/him inside her. It wasn't easy. She did feel swollen in the aftermath (and wished she wasn't such a textbook case but different from those other women he'd known), as if everything inside her had expanded with the tremendous pleasure.

"You haven't done this before either," he said, helping her, evincing not the slightest shred of reluctance or hesitation as he held her steady, opened her up (she looked away, shamed) and began insinuating himself into the tightened interior of her body. "Hurt?" he asked.

It took her a second or two to answer because she was still worrying over the fact that he must think her hopelessly inexperienced and boring. But he couldn't think that or he wouldn't be keeping on with all of it.

"No." She shook her head slowly back and forth. "It doesn't hurt." She braced her hands on his shoulders, thinking he looked entirely different at this range; staggered by her body's compliance (it didn't hurt, nothing hurt), by its awesome hunger. Opening her mouth over his. God! To have him touch and hold her, even if it was pretending. This was real because she was there and so was he. And creating the most sensational feeling inside her, working on a rhythm that sent her gliding up and down along a course of liquid pleasure while he held the hair away from her face with such tender-seeming hands, treating her so nicely, so gently, taking so much time with her. Frank never would.

"Baby, you're good." He smiled up at her, his hands slipping into place over her breasts again. "Don't ever let anybody tell you you're not good."

Slowly riding up and down, her head flung back arrogantly, thinking how different this was. Not the same sort of hammering, intense pleasure that he'd given her with his mouth and tongue. This was good because she was making the effort to return some of what he'd given her. A nice feeling. Pleasant, containing no panic. Moving because it seemed the right thing to do, because his face was shining with pleasure. Then, changing, his features becoming distracted, his hands moving up from her breasts to her shoulders as he now began to move; the movement of his hips sending him high, hard inside her, creating his own new rhythm she couldn't

105

follow, could only receive. She was suddenly separated from him, no longer involved. And cried out
involuntarily, but he kept going. She was galvanized,
immobilized. Understanding something, learning
something about herself, feeling stretched, taken.
It hurts now but it doesn't it does and it doesn't
and I can't get out of it now tomorrow I'll wish I
was dead but there's nothing I can do about right
now.

Mike kept one hand on her shoulder and let the
other delve down, slipping in, scoring a bullseye,
rubbing. Sidonie. You're too much, thinking once
was the whole shot. Once isn't all, baby. I can
make you come and come.

She felt like a torture victim, a victim. She'd
wanted to know. Well, now I know, she thought,
Michael pumping inside her his fingers rubbing
making her groan at the inflicted pleasure, her
fingers sinking into his sides as he picked her up,
carried her to the edge of a precipice and then, with
all his casual strength, his knowing skill, shoved
her over. She was lost, left to dangle like a puppet
held firmly in place inside and out as he bore down
on her shoulders—she could feel his fingers bruising
—upthrusting higher harder, coming. She'd never
actually been aware of the flow, the sudden flooding
inside. But she was acutely aware of Michael coming
inside her now. She felt every bit of it. That, then
the softening, shrinking and final withdrawal, leaving her empty-bodied, pulsing, collapsed in a dampened heap on his chest while he praised her, praised
the parts of her, putting his words to her parts

making her wish he wouldn't, calling her "baby," calling her "beautiful."

You do like me, don't you? You must like me to want me to feel good, to say the things you do.

He smoothed her hair, holding her, caressing her while she cried, feeling mortified by her so-unpredictable emotions; repeatedly kissing her cheek and trying to wipe away the tears.

"Hey, don't!" he crooned. "You said you wanted to know. Now you do."

SIX

Do I? Know, what do I know? I've done it finally, about all there is to do. All that time thinking it was something about Frank, the way he was with me. But it wasn't. It's me. I *think* it's me. And that has to mean there's something wrong with me. Blaming him when it wasn't him at all. I wish I were at home right now. I need to think. About everything. Here I am with this man who has to think I'm—what? Why did I have to start crying? It's so humiliating. Crying like a baby because my body can do some things and like them and not others. My head can't take this. I never thought it was going to be this way. To want all the attention, the hands and the mouth, all of it but not being able to bear it all really inside, hating myself for being willing to climb around this man like some sort of silly monkey. How am I going to get out of here without making myself look like more of a fool than I already have?

She was silent for so long, he wondered if this

time she hadn't gone ahead and fallen asleep. Okay with him if she had. He was happy as hell just holding her, stroking her bottom. Christ! What a body! I could lie here forever with my hands on you, breathing you in. Smell better than any woman I've ever known. Taste better too. Half-way serious until I got your clothes off and then Bang! something going off in my brain. Like dying, seeing someone as perfect as you are for "Honey," intimidating sort of getting close enough to touch and taste and get it all going with the one chick I've been looking for so damned long.

"Sidonie?"

"Hmm?" Her voice muffled, face hidden in his neck.

"You're good, babe. I can't believe how good you are."

"Why do you say that?"

"Because you are."

"I have to go to the bathroom. Where is it?"

"First on the right."

"Thank you." Her voice stiff, ludicrously formal, considering her naked state; considering the fact that she had, among other things, held this man's face between her legs.

His eyes followed her, watching, stunned by how absolutely right, how perfect she was. Jesus! I'm going to have to be careful. You're so good I can hardly react, for one thing. And for another, if I blow this and scare you off . . . That can't happen.

She felt enlarged, expanded as if he'd left part of himself lodged inside her to remind her of what could be done to her and her own inconsistent reactions to what he could do to her. She sat on the toilet, her toes touching together on the floor, leaning on her hands, feeling the soreness when she experimentally tightened her muscles. She rubbed her eyelids gingerly (mindful of her eye-makeup), then looked at the bathroom. All in shades of gray with the whitest towels, white bathmat, hamper. Shower curtain in chevron strips descending from charcoal at the top to pure white at the bottom. Gray-streaked marble basin with shining chrome fittings. All so neat and clean. I wonder who does his cleaning. Does he do it himself? She flushed the toilet and stealthily opened the medicine cabinet. Everything lined up, like rows of tin soldiers. Attractively bottled cologne, a brand she'd never heard of. How do I get out of here? If only I was drunk. Then tomorrow I'd be able to make excuses, tell myself a lot of lies about how I didn't know what I was doing so it isn't really my fault any of this, I can't be blamed. But I knew all the way. And I like this man so much but you don't start liking somebody who picked you up in a bar. But what he did, that, it was fantastic. And surely you don't do those things unless you feel something. Somehow, I've got to get my clothes and get out of here. I'm sore. Maybe it'll all collapse. What did Claudia say? Prolapse? My God! Is this the way it happens? Too much sex. I'd die having everything collapse inside, having to have surgery, be in a hospital, all sewn up.

I wish you never had to grow up, could stay

little forever, enjoying such simple things; not concerned with touching, loving. Encased in the private selfishness of being a child, greedily taking pleasure from rare moments of freedom; of diving into cool water on a hot July day; of cotton candy at the circus and holding your breath so excited when the trapeze artists swing way out up there at the top of the world with no net, nothing to save them if they fall. And the clowns. Doing crazy things. God, to laugh at something as uncomplicated as a clown! The excitement, the purity of every reaction. No need for analyzing the meanings of the words you hear, responding totally to parental, adult authority, accepting the yesses and no's of the what-you-can-do and what-you-can't. Not having to think beyond the primitive wants and needs. No sex. A small body as chaste and hairless as a toy. A glass of lemonade in August. So cold and tart, your teeth feeling gritty with the lemon tang, the acidity. Nothing cleaner, more satisfying. Maybe I'm a lesbian. Maybe I've been one all this time and didn't know. Who was there to tell me? Imagine blaming Frank because I could hardly ever come making love with him. Finding out now—so shaming—that I probably can't, not that way, with a man inside of me. It's a feeling but the awareness stays, interfering with whatever potential pleasure there might be. I wish I was a child, the way I used to be. Being grown, being a woman, I don't know what it is, how to be. Looking right on the outside, the way a woman's supposed to look. But inside, me inside. I still feel nine years old. And I miss the clowns. I have to go back in there. I wish I didn't have to, could just evaporate, vanish like steam.

She went back. He was still there on the sofa, looking so good. Black black hair and the bluest eyes. A wonderful face. All angles and shadows and someone hidden behind, someone I don't know. But your face makes me go soft inside, makes me absent-minded, sitting down beside you (like we were old friends), impulsively kissing your cheek. "I'd better go home now."

"Oh, not yet." He lifted his head, raising her breast, kissing her nipple. "Don't go yet," he said, his hand lingering on her breast, his mouth smiling up at her. "We haven't talked. Stay awhile. Come lie down with me. I love holding you."

Love, he used the word love. His words like verbal magnets, drawing at the iron inside her, bending her, making her sigh with confusion and renewing desire and a terrible longing to see if he'd use that telling word again in reference to her. He gathered her against him like a long, malleable cushion, placing a lot of small (affectionate?) teasing kisses on her mouth, his hands so nice; comfortable, but arousing too, finding their way up and down her back and arms, around over her breasts.

What am I doing, giving him back these small sweet kisses, liking having our faces so close together your features eyes are a blur, but so good the nicely-dry sweetness of these kisses, being cuddled without being hurried, hurried into opening my legs to be injected. Knowing, afraid now, my God, nothing

113

happens when I am. He isn't even hard. Just warm and good to put my hand between his thighs and hold him, fill my hand with the difference between you and me. I hated touching Frank. But this isn't the same. I feel like crying again.

"This is so nice," she said, her voice deep and suddenly husky (Is that *my* voice?). "You're being so nice to me. Really."

"Sidonie." He smiled a dazzling smile, his fingers playing with her hair in a way that seemed to be telling her how much he liked her. "You're so good, babe. I love the way you look, the way you feel. It's almost too much, intimidating."

That word again.

"Intimidating? I'm not *trying* to give that kind of feeling."

"Hey, I know that." He kissed her nose, her chin, his hand returning to her throat. "It's just a whole lot more than I expected. You know? Stay a little longer. You don't have to go yet. Come into the bedroom, we'll be comfortable."

"All right."

She didn't really want to go home. Not if he was going to keep on cuddling her this way, as if it made him feel good too; made him happy. She felt better, more quietly happy for these few minutes than she ever remembered feeling. She'd been inspected and not yet rejected. And wondered why, what it was about him that could make her feel so uncertain one minute, so profoundly happy the next. He did seem to like her, smiling so engagingly, giving her those loving little kisses, hugging her, cradling her to his body so endearingly.

The bedroom. All four walls covered in draperies. The bed huge, with eight feather pillows. And campaign chests in white lacquer, everything else blue: sheets, carpeting (thick, luxurious, shaggy), draperies. White lamps and a wonderful blue-white-green painting of sea and grass, spotlit on the far wall so that lying in bed you could enter into the depths of the painting. An image conducive to dreaming, peacefulness. She was impressed by the objects he'd chosen to surround himself with; the almost-casual opulence of the smallest details.

"You have very good taste," she said, as he tugged her down on that vast bed and rolled over and over with her, laughing. Ending up on top of her. Like a children's game.

"Oh, Michael," she sighed, "let down on me. It feels so good."

Heavy and warm and so solid, his weight from her shoulders to her thighs where he lay between her legs and her hands wouldn't reach all the way to where she wanted them to go because she had a sudden craving to clutch at his bottom, the curving, satisfyingly solid flesh under her hands; so wrapped her arms around him instead, some simpler part of her immeasurably comforted by his bulk, his weight; gazing into his glittering blue eyes thinking, You're the best-looking man I've ever known. If you loved me I could be so happy just to hold you on me this way, hold and hold you, sleep in your bed and wake up in the morning close to you, your arm around me all heavy and sleeping, warm, warm.

"Don't go home," he said, resting his cheek against hers. "Stay. I want you to stay. I'll give you breakfast in bed. I'll love you and feed you and feel so great waking up next to you. Nobody calls me Michael."

"Shouldn't I?"

"*You* should. I love it. The way your voice sort of cracks when you say it. I'd love to hear you say you love me."

A bullet shot through her from groin to brain and she shivered. This is a strange, dangerous game. I don't know what's real and what's merely a part of the game.

"I love you," she whispered. It wasn't at all difficult to say.

"*Jesus!*" He closed his eyes and went tight, hard all over, his mouth fastening to hers.

This is such a lovely way to play, she thought, searching his mouth, as if she might find more words hidden there, only waiting for a chance to be used. Feeling her hunger growing again; his sweetness and words making her crave having him inside of her; her legs bending either side of him, the muscles tensed with expectation and wanting and fear of failure. It's kind of you to say I'm beautiful. The things you say. Are they real? Do you mean them? Am I someone who could be special to you? Do you like me?

"I want to," she said in that hoarse, husky voice, feeling him butting gently against her. "But I don't think . . . It's something about me." Her face burned telling this stranger so private an intimacy.

"What's 'something about you?' " he asked, so confident and good to look at like a candy store window filled with every appetizing thing any child could ever want.

"I like it. But the feeling . . . the feeling's not the same, not as good. Not like, you know. The other way." Oh why? Why can't I just stop talking and pretend?

"What did you two do?" he asked, getting a disagreeable image of this ex-husband of hers. "Tell me! You're not hung up on talking about it, are you?"

"I don't know if I am or not. I've never talked about it. I feel stupid."

"Come on," he urged. There's nothing I can't do for you, baby. I can wind you like a clock, open you like a door, turn you on like a tap. I *know* you.

She took her eyes away from his, looking at the seascape. "He'd just . . . do it, you know. And then, afterward, he'd make me come." She grimaced, hating the memory as much as she'd hated the reality, as much as she hated telling about it.

"How?"

"With his hand. It used to make me feel terrible. As if he was doing me an enormous favor, something he'd have preferred not doing. I'd have to show him where and how. He couldn't ever seem to remember, fumbling around . . . Every time it'd be the same, making me feel so depressed. Like a

117

mechanical exercise. And after, I'd feel like death, so depressed and . . . I don't know."

"It takes a little practice," he said thoughtfully. "I gather the two of you didn't do any of that."

"How do you 'practice,'" she said angrily, "with someone who makes you feel ugly? Who doesn't even notice if you've got clothes on or if you haven't? Do you have any idea how it feels growing up believing you're all right, even pretty, then living with a man who doesn't even *notice* you? Doesn't *see*. It made me feel old. And ugly. You can't *talk* to someone like that, let alone try to tell him what you want, what makes you feel good and what doesn't!"

"Why'd you stick with him then?" he asked reasonably.

"Habit! I don't know. I thought that was the way it was supposed to be. Doing the housework. And the rest of it when *he* felt like it, not when I did. How was I supposed to know what to expect? Nobody told me."

"And now, because you didn't come with me inside you, all by yourself without a little help, you think something's the matter with you." He looked into her stricken eyes, waiting for an answer.

"Well, yes."

"That's crazy. That's really crazy. It takes a little effort to get the whole thing humming. But you'll buy something being wrong with you just because you haven't had a chance to find out yet where you're at."

"I know I'm stupid."

Why did I say that? I didn't mean it. I don't think I'm stupid. I'm something. But not stupid.

"You're not stupid," he confirmed. "You just don't know. That's a whole other thing. You're not hard work, you know, Sidonie. *Easy* turning you on, making you come. Easy. Like a dream, babe. What're you worried about?"

"Do you go through all of this with every woman you meet?"

"Sure. And I never get out of bed! I go through all this with someone I want to get to know better. Not every chick I meet."

"You want to know me?"

"Believe it!"

"But why?"

"You want to know *me?*" he countered.

"Yes," she said, though her brain said, You have to think I'm no one special, just somebody you picked up in a bar. So why would you want to bother getting to know me? I want you to want to. I'd just like to know why.

"Let's do some finding out about what's right for you," he said, brushing his mouth back and forth against hers. "Nothing wrong with being oral, sweetheart. And you're very oral."

"But I like having you inside me," she said quietly, discomfited. "It's only that I never seem to get as excited as I do, as I did the other way."

"We'll work up to it," he said, awing her with his unshakable confidence. "Stop worrying and get into it, get with the feeling."

119

"How did you get to know so much?" she asked seriously.

"I've got a few years on you. Jesus, you're good! If head's your trip, don't worry about it. I love it. You turn me on so goddamned hard!"

I must, she thought, very aware of just how hard. His mouth covering hers, his hips rocking against her. Her appetite rushing back; an expansion of receptivity. His mouth on her breast, sucking at her, his fingers inside her vibrating. The most extraordinary sensation, impaled on his hand that was reviving the need, the heat, sending her breathless and greedy. She loved this, *loved* it; dragged past thinking, worrying, caring. By his mouth sucking at her here, then here, his hand there, the other wedged down there, fingers thrumming rapidly inside her, the fluttering hummingbird beat of wings.

If I don't fuck you good, fuck you crazy, baby, I don't know you. And I *know* you, know *you*. Spreading her legs, keeping a close watch on her face as he moved in; aware instantly he was losing her. .

"We need a pillow," he said, inspired; grabbing one of the pillows, placing it hurriedly under her hips. Experimenting to find the feeling, keep her in it. "How's that?" he asked.

"Better. But I still can't feel you the way . . ."

"This way," he said, lifting his left leg over hers, all the while maintaining the connection. Then, trying again. Knowing at once he'd found the perfect play. A long, slow, careful thrust that—at the apex —had her caught. "That's it, isn't it?" he asked

120

her softly, seeing the impact registering on her features.

Her lips parted to make delirious sounds as she rode along the length of such a hard pleasure inside and out; riding him; his arm under her holding her crushed, holding her still while he dived deep, riding.

I want the whole feeling, all of it, everything, the biggest. She reached for his hand, biting into the web between thumb and forefinger, then one by one, his fingers, tasting each of his fingers until his hand was wet—her chest and shoulders burning—holding his fingers; both their bodies moving in convulsive haste.

It's happening, happening, everything I ever wanted happening have to hold you so hard while it's don't stop don't stop I'm going how we look how we sound don't stop Oh I love you for this love you Michael Quinn, Michael Mi

You beautiful I want you to feel so good make you hotter happier than you've ever been Jesus I love it the way you look the heat of you flushed in the throat your breasts flushed kissing my hand sucking my fingers Oral Jesus! Are you good good, beautiful baby wet and hot tight around me hot good come baby hold you make your bell ring while you God! You're beautiful coming making you look at the way you come all wild wild breathing hard harder little sounds like sobs I love you if you beautiful baby I'm going to come so hard in you so

What else could you teach me about me? All

121

kinds of things. You make my ideas seem so absurd. You make part of *me* absurd, as if you might laugh at the things that frighten me. But I like looking at you. If you were mine . . . I wish I could sleep every night for the rest of forever all snuggled up to you. Feeling so easy, never feeling with anyone the way I feel with you.

"Who are you, baby? Tell me who you are."

"I'm just ordinary. There's nothing to tell. Nothing very interesting."

"No way! You're fabulous, sweetheart. I could . . . Come on, tell me."

"Michael, I can't. Tell me about you."

The opening. The timing seemed perfect.

"There's this film I've always wanted to make," he began. "I've had the screen rights for years. True story about this guy's wife. Married three weeks. She goes to the bank to cash a check. Standing in line, right? These three dudes come in with masks, the whole number, to hold up the bank. One itchy guy. The guard makes a move and this guy fires. Hits this girl right in the head. Kills her instantly. Bang! A freak accident.

"The thing is, here you have these two people who go through all kinds of gut-aches and hassles, each alone. Finally finding each other. And some moron with a gun stamps The End all over it. You'd be great. I can *see* you. To do one decent film, Sidonie. One worthwhile film. I wouldn't care after that if I never did another goddamned thing in my whole life if I could just once make a quality flick. And, baby, I *know* you could do it."

"Are you asking me to make a movie?" She leaned on her elbow and looked at him, disbelieving. "One of *those* things?"

"Shit! Nothing like that. A real movie. About two people. A very straight flick. Simple, no tricks. Some love scenes, sure. *Real*, though. No crapping around. I'm so sick of the tricks, the weird, gimmicky stuff. A for-real movie. I swear to God, it'd be beautiful. I know a guy could write the best score. Know the right cameraman too. One of the best."

"Why on earth would you want to put *me* in a movie? I'm not an actress. I never even used to be able to memorize nursery rhymes."

"What if I say you can? What if I say I know you'd be outasight on film? And as far as the love scenes, we'd do them with a skeleton crew."

"I could never make love to somebody in front of other people. I'd die! I don't know how those girls can *do* it! I *couldn't*."

"Baby, you *could*. Three, maybe four weeks of shooting. Keep it simple. Some good outdoor stuff in the park. The interiors and then the bank for the ending. God, the ending. I can see it. Her eyes, then . . . It's tough trying to describe the visuals. But it'd be something we could all be proud of. Your voice is perfect. You wouldn't have any problem at all delivering lines. Wouldn't even have to use body makeup on you." He looked down at her, his thumb flicking her nipple. "Just clean, the way you are right now."

"Michael, no. Taking my clothes off, pretending

to make love to somebody. Who? That jerk, that kid? Never!"

"I'd give you five bills a day and five percent of the gross," he offered.

"What does that mean?"

"It means if the picture really cashes in and makes a whole lot of profit, you're going to be one sweet mama with a whole fistful of bucks."

"You're crazy!" she said, unsmiling. "Nobody in his right mind would pay to see me."

"The hell they wouldn't! Come on over here with me!" He took hold of her hand and tugged at her, towing her across the room to stand in front of a full-length mirror. "Look at you, babe!" He moved to one side, studying her. "Beautiful jugs. All that fucking gorgeous red hair. Even red here," he ran his fingers lightly down her belly. "Shit! You're perfect! I knew it the minute I saw you."

He directed her back to the bed.

"Would you just *think* about it?" he persisted. "Would you maybe consider it if I could find someone you like to play it with you?"

"Michael, listen! Tonight, what happened, you know, I've *told* you . . . I couldn't do all this in a *movie*."

"Would you do it with me in a movie?"

"With *you*?"

"Right. With me."

"Make love to you in a movie." She lay down and looked at the ceiling. "I like you. A lot. But a movie . . ." She turned towards him. "I can't believe you're serious. I mean, if I take you seriously,

people—me—I'll think I'm some kind of mental
defective or something. It all sounds so unreal.
You don't have to promise you'll put me in a movie
just because of all this. I'm . . . I've loved all of it.
I really have. I've never liked anything more. I
mean, you don't have to say a lot of wild things
thinking you're going to make me feel better or
something." God, I want to go home! This is
science fiction.

"Hey! I'm serious. For real. I'll give you a contract, the whole deal. Everything legit, in writing.
Real cameras. With film in them. Wardrobe. The
whole shot. The screenplay's already written. I'll
give you a copy. Take it home with you, read it.
You're *right* for this. You read it. If you think you'd
like to do it then we'll start things rolling. With
luck, we could get the whole thing put together and
out on the street by the first of the year. But the
flick's got to have the love scenes. Got to. I'm so
fed up with seeing cop-out flicks. The whole in-
dustry treating everybody like twelve-year-olds. I
mean, if I go to see a flick and I'm getting right into
it with the people up there and they start making
out, I want to know how they react to each other
making out. I don't want a tight closeup on the
chick's face while he's down there pretending he's
turning her on. I want the whole shot, see it all.
Because that's when you *know*. That's when you
really get into what's happening between those two
people, when you find out what kind of people
they are and how they relate to each other. The
rest of it, the dialogue, the sets, it's all dressing.

But the truth, the *truth* is how the two up there respond to each other making it, *loving*. Somebody's got to make a movie with a decent story, believable people and show how it is. But beautifully. And real. For-real lovemaking. To let everybody get involved, all the way involved. We're *not* twelve-year-olds, we're people wanting to know something more, see it played out. I want it when I see a flick. Other people do too. I know I'm going to do this movie someday. I'd like it to be now. And nobody'll ever be more perfect than you are to play Honey. When that chick dies at the end of this flick, I want every goddamned cat in that theater to feel they just lost the chick of their lives. I want the chicks bawling like babies because Honey's such a gas, such a nice, together chick. I want to take love, make it for the audience, show it and get them involved right up to their eyeballs. I know it's right. It'll work."

"You really believe that, don't you?" She was strongly impressed by his fervor.

"That's *it* for me, Sidonie. For me, the trip's a movie. Maybe once I've done something I really *feel* about, I can get into other things. I feel all kind of blocked right now; sewn into making rotten, tasteless flicks, working with assholes like Beau because it's a set gig and the bread just comes barreling in. You know? We all get tied into things, situations we don't like all that much but we're afraid to move because outside, away from what we know, what we're used to, it might be worse. A lot worse. Do this for me, babe. Do it! Trust me. I'm not working a con, trying to take advantage or do some kind of weird number on you. I know you're a nice chick, a straight chick. But you're so *right* for this. And making the flick is what's right for me. I'm no actor. Not any more than you are. But I believe. I believe if you take two people, make them real, give them real things to say and do, you can reach other people and get them into feeling right along with you. If you say you will, I'll go it with you. I need you for my movie. You're the one. Nobody else is right the way you're right."

"You're very convincing." His whole being seemed to be begging, urging her to accept. It gave her the oddest feeling in her chest: a choked-up mix of wanting to laugh and cry (laugh mostly because there was a preposterous element to all this), her heart skipping crazily, uncertainly. "I'll read it," she said, elated and scared to death. What am I getting myself into?

"Baby!" he laughed, taking hold of her. "I swear to God, I promise you, it'll be so beautiful. Everybody who sees this will fall in love with you. Trust me! I give you my word I'll make you beautiful. You won't be sorry."

Is this the way you fall in love? she wondered. Is this how it feels? With pounding in your throat and wanting to believe so badly? And hunger. Oh God, save me from my appetites, my hunger! Let this be real. I could be happy if this was real because nobody's ever treated me as important. In any way. Nobody's ever thought of me as beautiful, or forced me in front of a mirror and said, Look, look!

Don't be lying, Michael! If you lie to me, I'll die. Because I can't help myself, I believe you. I don't want to, but I do. I'm always going around believing people. But you think I'm good enough to put into a movie.

"I'll read it," she said again, trying to think what it would be like being in a movie. She couldn't. There was just a vague sort of interior agitation at the prospect of it. And a definite interior agitation generated by his urgings—the ones contained by his words, and the ones contained by his hands, his mouth, his body going hard. Because of wanting her. Wanting me this many times in one night.

"You'll love it," he said, leaving her confused as to whether he meant the one thing or the other.

Either way, she closed her eyes and leaped right in.

"Do it again!" she murmured. I need you to love me.

SEVEN

He wanted her to spend the night. But she couldn't. She wanted to be home, alone; to consider the day and the events of the evening. So after another lengthy lovemaking session that left her feeling like a Channel swimmer who'd crossed both ways without resting, she got dressed and then waited while he threw on a pair of jeans and a sweater.

"I'll walk you out to your car." But not before he'd presented her with a blue-bound copy of the scenario, handing it to her with all the profundity and gravity of someone entrusting Magna Carta into doubtful hands.

He kissed her a lingering goodbye, then stood in the road until she'd driven away. She glanced into the rear-view mirror to see him waving. That's that, she thought, curious about the bound pages lying heavily impressive on the seat beside her. I'm off home with a movie script. Yet, with him beyond her immediate range, everything seemed fantasylike.

Her having a film script. Her being on her way home at nearly four in the morning. Having bared and opened herself to everything sexual she'd ever imagined.

Her doubts increased with every yard of distance she was putting between them. By the time she was inside her apartment, she'd stopped believing. And wondered how it had been possible to believe so completely words spoken at mouth-to-mouth range, yet to disbelieve with equal intensity once alone on her own. All unreal. Things to be said because flattery was part of making the other person feel good. Heaven to have someone so attractive make fantastic love to you, all the while declaring you good enough, beautiful enough to be a movie star. But it wasn't the sort of thing you came home believing. Was it?

Climbing under the shower, she thought, I can handle this. I can. She felt satisfied. Down to the bones satisfied. There's nothing wrong with me. This new satisfaction seemed to act as cushioning, covering what had, before, felt like too many harshly glaring inadequacies. And now that she knew something more about her own capacities, what did that make Frank? Well, it made him—from the vantage point of appeased hunger—clumsy, insensitive, and totally lacking in skill.

There's not a damned thing wrong with me. It was you all the time, Frank. If I got fat and lazy, it was only because you never noticed, so what difference did it make?

Wrapped in a towel, she sat on the edge of the tub,

thinking; remembering the giddy wickedness of her first forays naked through the house. So positive Frank would see, be aroused, bend her backward in passion. He didn't even look up from the computer manual. Deflated, she'd climbed into one of her favored girlhood granny gowns and sought solace in a book.

I hid away so many feelings, pretending to myself they were transitory, unimportant. Spending days reading. Reading poetry. Reading Anne Sexton and thinking yes, yes, that's exactly how it is. Reading old, yellowing paperback copies of Millay, wishing my love, my feelings could parallel Millay's. Poets using the fewest possible words to convey the largest, deepest meanings; the most intense emotions. Sitting down in the middle of vacuming those miles of wall-to-wall to quickly turn the pages, devouring the messages of these gifted purveyors of four-line agonies. Word pills. Take two and die. The love poems of Elizabeth Sargent. Fuck me again, I'm a poet. Sidonie read and reread them, greatly admiring the courage it had to take to admit to such dreadful spells of darkness; such spasms of doubt and dread. Capturing the miseries of the uncertain side of loving, the gripping knowledge of the permanent separateness of everyone.

She could read the words, absorb the meanings so deep they seemed to flow with her blood. All personal messages direct from the poets to her veins. But no answers. Only a stating and restating of the problems. Carl Sandburg saying happiness was a crowd of Hungarians under the trees with their women and children and a keg of beer and an accordian.

It *sounded* so right. Because there was so much implied simplicity and contentment. But you needed the rest of the crowd. And something more. Not to mention the children and the keg of beer and the accordian.

The poetry left her sighing as she carefully replaced the books and returned to push her way across the Sahara of carpeting, wondering why she wasn't able to be content with the one Hungarian she did have; with the house and the chores requiring her attention.

Because, damn it! there was no return. No one telling me, You're good. You're beautiful. You make me feel so goddamned good. No one showing it. And that's the way I thought it should be. There was no way I could have gone on indefinitely, coping with the downs, the hunger, the put-downs, thinking that was all. And now, in one night, I've found out about things you had eight years to inform me of, Frank, but never took the trouble to try.

She got into bed and lay in the dark of this bedroom, this new living place she'd acquired, wanting to pursue her random thoughts but too tired to home in on them. So she slept and dreamed monstrously sexual dreams. All of them starring a black-haired, blue-eyed man with very white skin and well-shaped, persistent hands and legs that held her gladly captive as he promised and plunged and promised her more, plunging deeper.

In the late morning, she awakened carefully, tentatively scouting the new day for signs of imminent depression. Cautious, alert to dangerous self-recriminations. But none to be found lurking in the doorways or hiding in the closet; none waiting to claim her. She'd expected to feel somehow reduced, demoralized because of the way she'd so shamelessly spread herself for this man who'd taken her off her barstool and put her down on her back; put her up astride his mouth. All she felt, reviewing that first outrageous encounter, was a stunning desire to do it all again. And again. Climb on and ride his mouth, his body, his fingers; ride into oblivion. Slaking the thirst of all those years of deprivation, the months of loneliness. Ride it out until the knots inside and the fat woman still hiding there were ironed out to perfection like those shirts of Frank's she'd toiled over so drudgelike and obedient. Ride me, let me ride you until I've stored up enough to last awhile.

She got up, dressed, drank her coffee, gathered the contents of the hamper and made her way down to the basement.

Aurora sauntered into the laundry room while Sidonie was dreamily cramming her clothes into the washer, the film script waiting on the sorting table, to lean against the rickety table saying, in her lazy way, "You're lookin' real swell. Sure've pulled yourself together the last coupla months, I'll say."

Sidonie smiled with equal laziness. "I've been dieting, exercising."

"Makes me wonder sometimes," Aurora nodded approvingly. "You wonder, you know, if folks really see themselves. I guess maybe they do after all."

She said several other mildly inquisitive things (all the while covertly eyeing the script) which Sidonie failed to properly hear or answer, then bustled off to put a roast in the oven.

In a state of smiling preoccupation and continuing self-satisfaction, Sidonie watched her clothes begin their voyage of soaping, rinsing and spinning, then sat down (God! The stiffness, the soreness!) to begin reading the script. Not hearing the washer when it shut itself off. Caught up in the dialogue, unable to shift herself away from it for several minutes until she realized how silent the room was. Then stood, yawning, to dump the load into the dryer; more yawning while the dryer hummed and her mind tricked back again to the previous night. God, God! Fascinated with the details, going over and over them like a snoop reading someone else's five-year diary.

She'd fallen asleep. And he'd gone out to the kitchen returning with a tray of sandwiches and a bowl of salad. It had seemed unbelievable to her, upon awakening and being presented with this array of someone else's efforts, that she could, less than one day after the end of her marriage, be sharing a meal with a man she'd just met; one she found so appealing she could scarcely think, let alone eat.

"You must be hungry," he said, settling down with a plateful of salad and half a sandwich.

"You'll play hell with my anorexia," she complained, looking at the heaped tray, startled when he began laughing loudly.

"Anorexia! Too much! I love it."

She laughed with him, delighted her small stab at humor had been so well received. She couldn't make herself unaware of him, couldn't fake an interest in food. He was real. She was there with him. He'd prepared a meal, brought it to her in bed (Frank in a million years would never do anything like that) and was there watching her, urging her to eat. And looking utterly entranced as she picked up half a sandwich. As if he'd never seen anything more marvelous or intriguing than the sight of her eating ham and Swiss on pumpernickel and drinking coffee.

For her part, every time she saw his mouth open— to eat, to speak—she wanted it to be opening on some part of her. Seeing his hand curved around his bowl of salad, she wanted that hand to be curved around her breast. I'm in italics, she thought. Underscore me. I'm lower-case letters, make me into words. I'm someone inside, make me me.

It was she who, having consumed her half sandwich and having waited out the time it took him to eat two sandwiches and a second bowl of salad, set the tray to one side and advanced on him with all the dedication and conviction of Boadicea leading her female forces into the fray. To kiss and caress him, trying to store up the pleasure derived from these actions—for future reference—, gladly bold in opening her body to receive him, although

135

still somewhat passively taking pleasure from the evidence of his. A man who wants me. Who'd want me all night and tomorrow too if I'd stay. Yet, though she reacted most strongly to him with her body, her head annoyingly filled with reservations she wished would go away. But it was all right. Everything was fine. She was participating voluntarily in an act that had previously been forced upon her for the most part. Certainly, looking back, it had almost always seemed that way. There'd either never been enough time to begin reacting or it was finished too soon and she was left with her illicit load of appetites that she folded up and tucked away much as she saved brown paper bags from the supermarket All neatly stacked and put away. And now Michael had discovered and pulled open that particular drawer, finding a use for quite a surprising number of those meticulously concealed cravings.

Michael. The clothes spinning round and round, tumbling inside the dryer, the laundry room all warm and sleepy-making. Michael. What it would be to have you love me! Still, it seemed impractical, childish to hope love could grow out of so classic an encounter. Was it possible love might emanate from viewing pornographic movies in some man's expensively appointed private viewing room? Maybe it was possible. You do love me. I just know it.

When he telephoned later that afternoon, her mind was still held captive in the dreamlike, non-real qualities of the night before and its ongoing afterglow. Like playing out some part she'd been assigned and wasn't in the least reluctant to perform. Better than trying to think up ways to stave off the loneliness every single night; better than almost anything. I'm not sure what I've always wanted, but I think you're it. I only wish I knew more. But how do you know about people? They're like serials: a new episode coming every time you turn around; filled with perilous surprises.

She accepted his invitation to dinner, unable to think of one good reason why she shouldn't. She bathed, got dressed and then sat down to wait for him, unwilling and unable to descend from the euphoria. Feeling good, feeling happy, not bored.

She'd read the script, liked it, and had come full circle back to believing him. There really was a movie and he really wanted to do it. But why had she complied so readily, saying I love you? Why not, though? If it pleases him to hear it, why not? I know it's not real. I can handle this. I'm a grown woman. Outside.

Still, for all she knew he might be a liar and a user, a clever consumer of gullible women like me. And way inside, to be truthful, the things we did last night, I feel they were kind of terrible; letting a man do those things to me, doing nothing to prevent any of it from happening, because I had to know. Maybe he only wants me to do this film, or maybe he offers it to every female he meets, or maybe he thinks I'm the type who'd take on two or three or maybe half a dozen. Like that girl in the film. On her hands and knees with one man under her, Beau behind her, another using her mouth.

Those men, all built like battering rams. And that girl, her body just absorbing all of it. Awful. I'd never do anything like that. I hope Michael understands that. I wouldn't do the things I did with him with just anyone. Or would I? Could I?

Frighteningly, it occurred to her she didn't really know what she was capable of doing. Oh God! *Am I the type who'd take on three or four, or a dozen?*

He came to the door with flowers. The sight of them made those funny things happen again inside her chest—that laughy-crying sensation—and she wasn't sure what to do or say.

"You look great!" He put his arm around her shoulder, closed the front door and propelled her into the living room. Appearing to believe he had the right to be doing these things. And he had, in some indefinable fashion, gained some sort of power over her. She wanted to say, Just wait a minute! Stop a minute! I have to think about what's happening. But there was no chance, no room.

Strange, all so strange. Too many different things happening too quickly; an assortment of feelings and none she could be sure of. Except being so high and happy. Like being little on her birthday. Reaching out eagerly to snatch the gifts out of every newcomer's hand, so anxious to see what was contained within the gaudy wrappings. Forgetting temporarily the letdown, the exhaustion at the end of the party. Caught up in the opening-moment feelings, all emotions made magically new.

Over dinner, he held both her hands and said, "I've got the ball rolling. Cameraman's all lined up.

I'm scouting locations, working on permission from a bank downtown. I figure we should shoot the closing scenes in a real bank. We need the coldness, the starkness of a big bank." She couldn't stop him, couldn't find any space between his words to say, But I haven't agreed to *do* this.

His words kept on coming, washing over her in an enthusiastic wave. She heard the sounds, gathered the sense of their meaning, but found it exceedingly difficult to get her brain working. One voice in her head kept saying, I can handle this. And another, more reasonable one contradicted, insisting, This is already out of control. Open your mouth and tell him he's going too fast.

"Have you looked at the script yet?" he asked her.

"I read it this morning. It's very good." She wondered if he wore contact lenses. She'd read about tinted lenses that could change the color of your eyes. "Do you wear contacts?"

"Contacts?" He laughed. Some of the things she said were from nowhere. "No. I'm twenty-twenty. Why? That's kind of a weird question. Do you?"

"No. I was just wondering."

"*Your* eyes are a trip. You're not uptight about last night, are you?"

"Some. I wouldn't want you to think I do that sort of thing . . . indiscriminately."

"I know that, babe."

"How do you know that?"

"Maybe it's just that I don't want you to be that way. But I could tell by your reaction when Beau

139

started suggesting we should all split to his place. No way you were going to go."

"I'm not very smart. I mean, I'm not all that worldly." She groped for words, not quite sure what she wanted to say. "I don't know about how I am because the opportunities for finding out were never there. I wasn't allowed any. Then, suddenly, eight years later I knew I couldn't keep on indefinitely, pretending I didn't know my life had stopped, that I wasn't going anywhere. All at once I was angry and older and awfully ignorant about a lot of things. Sex mainly. I'd lost whatever identity I'd had to begin with. Now, here I am, one day later. Divorced. With you. And I can feel myself getting involved and I know Aunt Claudia would jump all over me, warning me not to. I'm supposed to be having a good time, not getting involved. But I *am* getting involved. I don't have any techniques or whatever it is women are supposed to have because while all those other women were getting their routines all put together and tested, I was out there in my little suburban cubbyhole doing laundry and cooking, playing the happy little housewife for someone who was primarily interested in keeping me down, as if I was some sort of uprising about to happen."

"What're you trying to say, babe?" he asked quietly.

"I think I'm trying to tell you that I'm not the way I look on the outside. I mean, I didn't always look this way. I've only lately . . . grown into it. Aunt Claudia calls me a latent type. I'm only just beginning to grow into myself. Something like that.

I haven't known a lot of men. Frank. You. I didn't go out with all that many boys, or do a lot of fooling around. I went to the neighborhood school because my mother was into liberalism and equality. For other people. Not for herself. She wanted me to get right down there with the other kids and be one of the gang. Except that every time I came home from school, she'd be there reminding me of my background, of the fact that I could never really *be* one of the gang. One contradiction after another.

"And then, in high school, I was too tall and too skinny and awkward. I hated the way I was. I wanted to be like all the other girls. I wanted to stay little.

"The boys didn't scare me half as much as my mother's warnings about the 'possibilities.' The worst things that can happen. Every time some boy approached me and we'd start to talk, halfway through, that long speech about 'possibilities' came back to me and I'd start looking at the boy as a potential threat instead of just a boy who was interested. And that killed it off. I didn't have very many dates. Not because I wouldn't have gone if I'd been asked but because I'd set some sort of precedent somewhere along the line and didn't know how to change what I'd started. I got teased a lot. Called 'her ladyship,' because my mother was titled, you see. English, with a title that came to her because of some kind of hereditary accident. No male progeny. Something. But the thing was, she'd sent me off to be one of the gang, yet she'd robbed me in advance of any real chance of fitting in by constantly reminding me

of who I supposedly was and the damned background
I was supposed to be living up to. Here I am now
and I feel as if I'd been voluntarily buried in ice for
the last eight years. Suddenly I'm defrosted—I *had* to
get out of that—and everything I used to know is
gone, finished. Inside my brain, I'm still twenty—
in too many ways, I think—and know about as
much as I did back then. I haven't yet managed to
figure out what people *do* out here. I don't know
how they get through their days, what keeps them
going, what makes them happy. I know I wanted
to be out here. But I don't know what I expected
to find. Now I'm getting involved with you. and . . .
I always wanted to be married. It was all I ever
wanted. To have a home of my own, children, someone I loved to share it with me. I didn't have it with
Frank. I tried to pretend I did. But I couldn't ignore
the truth: we had nothing. A lot of silences.

"I still want the same things. That's what's a little
frightening. I still want to be in my own home with
someone I love, having babies, cooking dinners,
talking together when the kids are in bed. Those are
the pictures I've always painted in my head. I don't
want to go to work in some store or office and fake
it some more, pretending that that's what I need and
want. Because it isn't, anymore than Frank was. Are
you stringing me along? Are you? I don't mind if
you tell me right now that that's the way it is, that
it's all casual. I won't mind. But *tell* me. Because
I want babies. And my own home again. The thing
is, I'm never going to be out there burning my
brassieres and demanding to be liberated. I'm happy

being part of something with someone else. I *am* programmed. I'd like not to be. But I don't know what to do in its place. And if that picture makes me happy, what's wrong with it? It's where Aunt Claudia and I part company. Her whole thing is telling me not to fly out and get myself stuck in another marriage that's nothing more than a replay of the first one."

"Aunt Claudia sounds like a heavy-duty chick," he said, toying with her hand. "She's trying to get you out into the world to do your thing, huh?"

"Use my potential. But my potential feels it ought to be making babies, cooking, being home somewhere."

"Maybe then that's what you should be doing."

"I would be, if I could."

"Well, listen, the film's for real. I want to get going with it. I don't know what else to tell you."

"I didn't say those things to get you to make commitments to me," she lied. She wanted him right then and there to ask her to run off with him and get married.

"You sure about that?" he asked.

"What do you mean?"

"Are you sure you're not laying down the guidelines? Cluing me in on how far you'll go, what you're after?"

"I'm only being honest. Is that bad?"

"Who'm I to say? It's a newy, that's all. I don't know a lot of chicks who come right out and say: This is what I am, what I want, what I expect. You're a whole new ballgame for me. What I wonder is how you can be so sure about where you're at. How do you know you're not reacting, saying you want all that because you've never done anything else? Until you've tried a few other gigs, how can you be so sure that that's your thing?"

"I can't be, can I? Don't try to scare me, Michael. It's bad enough having Aunt Claudia harping about my potential and my so-called intelligence."

"I'm not out to scare you, babe. What does that net me? What I want is your go-ahead on the movie. It's everything to me and I can't do it without you."

"But why *me*?"

"Why *me*? Why anybody? Because I've got the money, the script, the know-how and the right woman. I'm willing to risk making a complete ass of myself by playing in it with you. Because there's no way otherwise you'd do it. Are you going to do it?"

"I guess so." I'm agreeing because if I don't, I'm afraid you'll go out and find some other woman and I won't see you again. This isn't right. Why am I doing this?

"Nice place," he observed. "Comfortable."

"I love *your* furniture," she said zealously. "They're the sort of things I've always wanted to have. But Frank was big on matched 'suits', he called them. You know, when you get six pieces of garbage for seven ninety-five and they throw in a couple of coffee tables or a tacky lamp for good measure."

"You're bitter as hell about him."

"*Am* I?" She looked very surprised. "Do you really think so?"

He put his hands on her shoulders and lust came down over her like a shroud. Desire was a weapon her body had begun manufacturing with all the haste and efficiency of a munitions factory.

"I dig your bed," he said against her lips, his hands on a tour of her arms. "Don't be bitter and uptight about a dead issue, babe. Pick up the pieces and go from there."

She couldn't answer, talk. How could anyone talk rationally having someone sliding his hands up and down the length of your arms, kissing your mouth, nibbling on your lower lip, making all the blood rush to your head, making your knees go wobbly and your stomach fluttery?

"It's really something." He smiled, throwing off his clothes so quickly she stood wondering how he'd managed it. "You're a whole other chick without your clothes." And as if to prove it, he withdrew her from her clothes as neatly and easily as slipping a new-laid egg out from under a chicken. Then lined her body up against his, his hands squeezing her buttocks as he beamed at her.

"Your ass, babe!" he laughed. "Jesus, what an ass!"

There's a feeling inside of me I don't like. It has to do with the way you talk, the way you talk to me, the way everything you do is somehow directed toward getting me into bed.

As she watched, he pulled off the bedspread, then stretched out on her bed, beckoning her to come,

145

to lay herself down beside him. And she didn't want to. But did. Because a persistent voice in her head kept saying, Love me, please love me. Value me. Want me for your life. I hate to be alone in the world, looking, hoping.

Frank never touched me there the way you do. When he did it was an ugly part of an ugly ritual. Stick in a perfunctory finger and get the kid oiled. In the beginning I was always wet. But after the first year, into the second, I started sneaking into the bathroom when your signals started, to apply Vaseline so it wouldn't hurt because nothing happened inside me anymore. Nothing. No feelings, always dry. Buying Vaseline feeling so dishonest, almost sinful. Feeling about it the way I used to feel at twelve asking the man behind the counter in the drugstore for Kotex. Always feeling there was something ignominious, befouling, asking a man for Kotex because he was a *man* and you were telling him right out loud that you bled every month and were probably bleeding at that very moment standing there asking in a tiny voice for your box of Super Kotex, please; wanting always to add, It's for my mother.

Michael, I get wet just listening to you talk. My breasts swell when you hold my hands. And inside, way down, everything contracts, then widens feeling so starved. Love me. I could always be wet for you, always empty without you.

Touching her, teasing her nipples hard, sliding his fingers around, over, in her, he felt high, hopeful; yet semierect, defeated by unexpected feelings crowding inside him, growing there for her. Looking for a moment at the panic on her face before he burrowed deep searching for the taste, the scent that had become immediately importantly recognizable to him as belonging only to her, hers uniquely. Honey in the flesh. Moving up, tasting her mouth, wanting her but finding all his impulses blocked.

"I want to be *in* there," he said despairingly. "God damn it!"

She looked alarmed. "What's wrong?"

"I told you last night. I'm intimidated."

She touched herself, then touched him, looking up at him with that vulnerable expression she'd had the night before, saying, "It doesn't matter, does it?"

"No, babe." What the fuck? I can keep you right up there all kinds of ways. But what *is* this? Shaken up, rattled, a flash image of Grace darting past him. He opened Sidonie's thighs and put his mouth where he most wanted to be, reassured by her response, the slow lift of her hips.

I can tell him it doesn't matter but it obviously matters to him, this is so sad. God, so sad! Putting your mouth on me. After one night, knowing the feeling now, it's all sad. I feel like your mother, Michael. Some strange, crazy sort of mother, holding your head between my hands while you suck on me the way I used to suck on navel oranges. A twisty, maddening kind of feeling.

"Don't worry," she whispered inaudibly, her body going insane. Breathing hard, drowning, gasping, "Oh, oh!" closing in on the feeling like some deranged huntress stalking the most elusive prey; closing in, in heat and dampness and held breath. Like dying. Climbing to the top of the highest building to throw your arms way out in the air, holding your breath while you stand there wondering how it's going to feel, then stepping off the edge, leaping into space, flying; knowing now how it feels, the air rushing out of your lungs, exhilaration and loss of control; body spinning, hurtling through space; whirling, turning, spinning, convulsed. Crying out. Clutching handfuls of air, clinging wetly to the last shreds of reason, completing the fall, spilling drunkenly into the eddying depths of a whirlpool.

"You'll do it, won't you, babe? For my sake?"
"I will. But I'm scared." Oh God, I'm so scared!
"Don't be, babe. I'll take good care of you."

EIGHT

"What're you doing?" he asked.

"You know what I'm doing. Nothing. Come over.".

He went, feeling cowardly. But in need. To prove something. Grace with her ways of making him feel he was copping out on responsibilities he hadn't known he had.

She prepared a late supper. And all the way through the meal, he scouted ways of telling her. But she'd already guessed.

"You've found another one," she said, setting down her fork with concentrated precision.

"I meant to call you this morning. But there's a lot happening."

"That isn't why you didn't call," she said quietly, picking up her coffee cup. "You just hoped I'd quietly die. Isn't that right?"

"No, that's not right."

Grace smiled knowingly, then drank some of her coffee.

"Don't pretend. You don't have to with me. I don't have many illusions. They tend to get lost by the time you hit forty. What's she like?"

"Let's not do that number, okay? I don't do it to you."

Always so calm. He found it unnerving. That calm and her way of knowing what he was doing when he wasn't sure himself.

"Serious?" she asked, still smiling.

"I don't want to talk about it, Grace. You're out of line."

"So," she said, setting down her cup. "No more two A.M. calls for a while, no unannounced surprise visits."

"I don't know," he said, chagrined. Yet starting to react, as he always did. Jesus, he'd been uptight! What the hell was it about Grace? No raving beauty. Not compared to someone like Sidonie. But something. That long neck and knowing look. And the heat underneath all that cool, slow exterior.

"Perhaps the occasional when-you-can-slip-in-a-minute visits," she went on, lighting a cigarette, exhaling leisurely. "I know that one. We've done that one before, too." She turned sideways to cross her legs. A small-boned, aristocratic blonde with hollows under her cheekbones and brown eyes that seemed to be constantly laughing at him. An elegant, flat-assed, tight-bellied, stingingly sarcastic woman who could shout lethal obscenities on the brink of coming.

He smiled, meeting her eyes.

"Old friends, old buddies," she smiled back. "Isn't that how it goes?"

"If you like." How the hell did she do it? he wondered. Every goddamned time. Off he'd go, convinced this time was it. End of the game. And she'd be there smiling when he came back. All cool, low-key. No fuss, no muss, no bother. Then wham! She'd hit him with a look and he was gone.

"This makes, what?" She attempted to run a mental tally. "Five or is this the sixth? What is it you think you're going to find, my love? Or are you aware you're looking?"

"This is different."

"Oh good!" She smiled again. "There are a few things I'd like to do knowing I'm not going to be interrupted."

"Don't hassle me, Grace. Your whole trip is being interrupted."

"So cock-proud, Mike! It's no great accomplishment, you know."

"And what're you? Cunt-proud? That's no big trick, either."

"Possibly not. It has to do, I'd say, with recognizing the truth when it hits you between the eyes. And with all those lost illusions. How are you getting on with your movies?"

She was homing in on him like an I.C.B.M. It made him sweat.

"Just fine. How's your interest rate?"

"Holding steady. I suppose you think it's a whimsical pastime of mine. My stocks represent my income. We're not all quite so lucky as you, darling.

I don't happen to have millions. And following the stock market requires a bit of intelligence. You should try it."

"You want money, Grace?"

"Not yours, darling. That's not what I want from you. You are so *basic*. I find it awfully difficult to separate your money from your means of manufacturing it."

"What d'you want?"

"Not a thing, darling." Composed as a statue, cigarette smoke curling upward through her fingers. Narrow kneecaps, swinging foot. She laughed suddenly, tossing her hair. "Shall we dance?"

"Jesus!" He exploded, jumping up, grabbing her wrist. "What you want," he said scornfully. "I've got what you want."

"Gently!" she laughed, reaching across the table to drop her cigarette in the ashtray. "Gently, darling. I'm old, you know. My bones are getting brittle."

"Old. Shit! You're forty-fucking-one. And your bones," he scoffed. "Your bones bend like rubber."

"Only for you, darling." She came up easily out of the chair, her body all sharp angles and sudden surprising softnesses. "Because you just have to keep coming back. I'm the one who keeps your furnace stoked for the others you feel so obliged to fall in love with."

"Shut up!" he whispered, both hands under her dress. Wearing nothing underneath. And her mouth a canyon. Falling into it like a parachutist. Picking her up and hurrying into her bedroom, to push everything off the chest of drawers and sit her on the edge of it so he could take out his rage, his self-disgust, his terror between her thighs while she twined her legs around his neck and pulled his hair, bucking and groaning, heaving her way into her decimating need for all his arrogance, all his anger, all his love.

As he threw her down on the bed, already fired to the bursting point, her fingernails bit into his neck and ears. Dragging him down by the hair, whispering, "Bastard, I love you," sending him berserk, making him sob, burying the pain in her narrow, enveloping body, making him cry out. "Grace! Do me, baby! I need you. Jesus! need you."

And she did. Like nothing, no one else. Dissolving his life, his dreams, his fruitless attempts at loving other women. Squeezing out the white-hot stream of passionate attachment that existed only for her. His love, his hate, his late-night, when-he-remembered-woman, his anchor, his hundred-and-two-pound, forty-one-year-old compulsion. Grace, this woman of shifting images, of hot and cold, weak and strong. He couldn't break her, couldn't break his endless need for her, couldn't escape the rapacity that took flame every time he saw her or heard her voice. She made no effort to keep him, said and did nothing to encourage him. Would never phone him. Would never make the slightest effort to hold him back. And he couldn't leave her alone, couldn't resist the lure of her clever words and unquenchable thirst. She could outthink, outsmart, outfuck him every time. And he loved and despised her totally.

"Admit you love me," she whispered, holding him trapped in her body. "Go on, admit it!"

The game, the game. Every time.

"I love you," he moaned. "Bitch! I love you."

"Not a bitch," she whispered. "And you know it. You'll never give in. Be nice, darling. I'm not angry loving you. Stop fighting. I've never tried to keep you, make you stay. You're the one, not me. I'd simply miss you if you went for good."

"Liar. Cunt. Liar."

"I love you."

"I'm in love with someone else."

"Not the same thing, darling. You know it's not. You'll still call me. At two or three in the morning. And I'll still be here."

"I'll marry her, Grace," he threatened.

"I'll dance at your wedding. And during the reception you'll be upstairs or outside somewhere with your pants down, fucking me. Give in! You could do worse."

"She's what I need," he insisted.

"For the moment. But I'm the one you call when the wanting goes wrong, and the need is doubtful. You'll kill it off one day, Mike. You'll go too far. One morning you'll wake up wanting me more than you've ever wanted any of them. It'll happen. And I'll be gone. It'll be too late."

"I can't help that. I can't!"

"You don't know, do you? No idea who you are, or what. Just proceeding, doing your 'thing.' It's been a long time and I know you so well. Fifteen years." She took a deep breath and something changed behind her eyes. "Finish me and go home, Mike. You depress me every time you start these new affairs. Fuck me and go home. Or go to your new one. But don't forget what I've told you."

"You'd never *let* me forget."

"You forget too many things, darling. I'm the one who married someone else to get away from you, to make it end. And you're the one who blew my marriage sky-high. *You*! Finish me! *Finish*!"

"What would you do if you had me?" he asked sourly. "Back then I was too young and Sue was in the way. I got rid of Sue but you were too old. You had to prove something with getting married. Now it's all coming even. And we're still where we were when we started. If you can't take me the way I am, let me off so I can have this new one."

"Is she young? Is she good? Are you teaching her everything I've taught you?"

His eyes were enraged. He lifted himself away menacingly.

"If you hit me, I'll kill you," she said softly. "Don't try it! Tell me! Does she melt for you, darling? Does she moan and quiver and love how you love her? Does she make you feel as good as I do?"

"Leave me alone, Grace."

"Then finish me and go home!"

"God!" he cried, his hands around her throat as he smashed all her jagged edges, reduced her and her softly sucking body to whimpering silence. "I wish to Christ I'd never met you!"

"You'll want me. You'll burn with it. And I'll be gone!"

He returned home to lie in bed staring at the ceiling, half of him wishing she'd die, the other half terrified at the prospect.

Throughout her next Sunday afternoon visit with Claudia, Sidonie debated telling her aunt about Michael, about the film, about her feelings on both. Finally, she decided it would be safe to tell a limited amount about Michael.

"That's smart work," Claudia said, subjecting Sidonie to one of her more penetrating visual examinations. "I thought you were looking a bit less fraught. You've lost those telltale circles under the eyes."

"I've always had circles under my eyes."

"Not *those*!" her aunt said impatiently. "There's a decidedly smudged look some women get about the eyes when they're sexually underprivileged. You've had them for years. I gather it's all very good."

"Wonderful!" God, I'm hopeless! "He's very nice," she added, hoping to temper her too-obvious enthusiasm.

"Wonderful?" Claudia smiled. Sidonie interpreted this particular facial display as mildly wicked. "And precisely *how* is he wonderful?"

"Oh," Sidonie's hand fluttered ineffectually through what was supposed to be a grand gesture but came across as simply agitated. "He's very good-looking, very . . . I didn't mean to imply he's extraordinary."

"Yes, you did. Tell me more!"

"I swear, I think you're some sort of thwarted madame. He's a nice man and I like him. That's all." He makes me feel peculiar about myself, makes me question my needs, my motives. I think I love him and hate myself for thinking it.

"He's a good lover. What more? Claudia lit a Sobranie and recrossed her legs, settling more comfortably into the Chinese Chippendale armchair.

"He's divorced, lives in the Park. He's in films. He evidently has a good deal of money. I just like him. I should've known you'd give me the third degree."

"Dear child, if you hadn't wished to dissect the man piece by delicious piece, you'd never have mentioned him in the first place. You're one of nature's more ingenuous females. What about him bothers you?"

"Nothing. I didn't say anything about being bothered."

"Darling, darling," Claudia shook her head, "you're such a dismal liar. You can't deceive me. You may have a legitimate problem and you may not. Tell me and then we'll decide whether or not you're to continue with this man."

"Of course I'm going to continue," she said too quickly.

"I see." Now Claudia looked plainly grieved. "You've gone ahead and done precisely what I warned you not to do: fallen for the first one to come along and tell you you're beautiful. I did warn you, Sidonie."

"I knew you'd do this. You don't understand."

"Do I not? Enlighten me then!"

"Why do I tell you things?" Sidonie mourned. "Every single time, some innocent remark I make gets blown into a full-scale anatomy class. I don't feel like dissecting Michael."

"Then you should not have introduced him into the conversation."

"You're so difficult! You love being difficult and contrary. I think you get some sort of perverted kick out of it. The things you expect me to tell you, show you!"

Claudia smiled again, leaning over to flick the ash from the tip of her cigarette. "I do," she admitted. "I get such a great deal of pleasure from you, darling. You're such an innocent. Utterly determined to end your days stuck somewhere in the suburbs, up to your armpits in dirty underwear and greasy dishes, with a gaggle of whining children hanging about your thighs. Can you truthfully tell me you'd be satisfied with that?"

"If I say I would be, you'll only start in on that business about my potential. My God, Claudia! So what? What good does any of it do me if I wind up alone? And will somebody please tell me what's so terrible about wanting children, a husband, doing the things I enjoy? I love those things. You make it sound as if being a wife and mother are the lowest forms of womanhood. I don't think so."

"You're not giving yourself any real chance to explore your own limits, Sidonie. You've simply latched onto the first good-looking, sexually competent man to come along. Because your first forays into the world have frightened you. It's not good enough! You haven't come this far to simply give up. It makes all your effort, your decisions senseless. You're most likely doing your utmost to rope this man into setting you up in another potentially stifling marriage."

Sidonie clasped her hands in her lap and said nothing. Because it was true. She was right. And what was worse, there was the film. She couldn't tell Claudia about that.

"Sidonie," Claudia said in a lower, less strident voice, "you can have a man, a child if you wish. But it isn't a part of the bargain that you give up your native wit, your independence. You've got to continue actively searching out your identity. The *role,* the assigned duties without thinking, without variation, it's what you ran from. I'm not deriding the possible virtues of being a wife and mother. I'm trying to point out that what is foolish is making an unhealthy alliance for the sake of getting yourself a child and a husband. Go home now, will you, darling? Anna's anxious to clear up in here and Jacob's due in half an hour. I'd like a few minutes to myself before he comes. You exhaust me, Sidonie. Sometimes trying to talk sense to you is like repeatedly smashing one's head against a brick wall simply because it feels so good when one stops. You take one step forward, then six steps back."

"If I'm so damned exhausting, why do you bother?"

"Because I love you. Because you could be a quite marvelous woman if you'd stop running scared at each new intersection, if you'd just once look at

159

yourself realistically and see yourself as you are instead of as a child, as someone second-hand because you've had a bad marriage. Come give me a kiss and go home. I'm getting a headache."

"Why does everything have to go according to your schedule?" Sidonie asked. "You know something? I have this incredible inclination to tell you to go fuck yourself. Now why the hell do you suppose I'd want to say something so *rude*?"

To her complete perplexity, Claudia erupted into hoarse, wheezing laughter, going on until tears were streaming down her face and she was choking on her cigarette smoke. Sidonie crossed the room to pound her on the back, then went to the bar to pour some ice water.

"Drink this!" She shoved the glass into Claudia's hand. "Crazy old woman!"

"Am I?" Claudia gasped, red-faced. "Got you to react with some fire, didn't I?"

"Christ!" Sidonie smiled. "You never quit!"

Claudia's arms went around Sidonie hard.

"I love you. Go, get growing, get your life to fit. Don't throw it all away for the sake of a few orgasms and a baby. You're worth so much more than that. Give me a kiss and go along home! But remember something, Sidonie! This isn't some sort of sadistic self-indulgent game I'm playing. You're important to me. I wish to God you could feel important to yourself."

Walking out confounded. A terrible need to cry. And guilt. Terrible guilt.

Damn you, Claudia, you reach right inside me with your small bejewelled hands and squeeze the hell out of everything in me. I wish I didn't love you, wish you didn't have this insane compulsion to drag me through all this soul-searching. Crazy old woman with your handsome men friends, your ultraperfect taste and your knowledge of all my weaknesses and fears. God, I wish you were my mother! I wouldn't be so screwed up right now if I'd had you kicking me through my life. Do you and Jacob sleep together? How the hell do you know so much?

Why did I say I'd do his movie? I said I would because I don't want him to stop making love to me. It's not a good enough reason for agreeing to take my clothes off and make love to him in a movie. For all kinds of people to see. Still, it's exciting sort of. The idea of it. The *idea* of it.

She arrived home in time to watch the local six o'clock news. Nothing. Without Walter Cronkite, without Eric Sevareid to make analyses, the news was unpalatable. Sitting staring at the TV screen crying because Claudia said a lot of really mean things.

If I did go back to school, what would I take? There's nothing I'm interested in. Except cooking. What I'd really like to do is take a cooking course. I wouldn't have to tell her what I was taking. I could just say I'm taking classes and not tell her any more than that. If I had a diploma, I would actually have the skills to open a restaurant.

Michael telephoned at seven-fifteen to say, "How

about some Chinese food and a little making-out?"

She felt like neither. And winced at his euphemisms.

"Michael, I'm really not in the mood. Do you mind?"

"Yeah," he said, keeping it light, but minding. "How about corned beef on rye, sour pickles and a lot of making-out?"

"I don't think so . . ."

"Okay. How about pita, dolmas, some shishkebab, boklava. And an hour or two of head?"

She laughed, sickened. He wasn't going to give up. And if she kept resisting, he'd use even uglier suggestions.

"All right," she gave in. "Come get me. But I'm warning you. I'm in a crummy mood. I went to see my aunt this afternoon."

He arrived wearing jeans, a ragged-elbowed navy turtleneck and a really ancient dufflecoat complete with toggles.

"Lousy enough?" he asked, hugging her at the door. "Look right to go with your crummy mood?"

"Close," she said, disengaging herself. For just a moment she felt as if she hated him. He was there when she hadn't wanted him to be. But not only could she not say no, she couldn't (despite his vocabulary) resist the blatant sexual invitation he offered.

"Come on in," she said. "I have to brush my hair and put on my shoes."

"What did auntie say to get you so uptight?"

For some reason, his reference to Claudia annoyed her.

"Don't do that! She's my aunt and I love her. You don't know her so don't refer to her that way." I've only known you two weeks, seen you five times. I've known her all my life. So shut up!

"Hey, hey!" He held his hands up palms outward. "Nobody's dumping on your aunt. I'm just trying to get you to spill what's bothering you."

"All kinds of things!" she replied hotly, flushing furiously.

"Okay, okay!" He smiled coaxingly, dropping to his knees to wrap his arms around her thighs and gaze up at her with a mock forlorn expression.

"Don't play with me," she said tiredly. "I can't . . . don't!"

Slowly he got to his feet and looked at her.

"What's the matter, Sidonie?"

What am I doing with you? she asked herself, suddenly unable to speak for the depression scratching at the edges of her mood like some sick animal trying to get somebody inside to open the door and let it in. You don't want me, need me. Not really, not for good. I don't like the way you talk or the things you say.

"Come on. What's the downer?"

"I want . . ." She stopped, fighting back tears.

"What?" he prompted. "What do you want?"

What I want. I want someone who loves me not for what I'll do for him but for what I *am*. And you're not the one. I know it. You're not the one because I don't know who I am so how can I find the one who'll want what I am?

"I don't know," she said in a small voice.

"I love you," he said, stroking her hair. "It'd be such a gas if we could get into telling each other the real feelings, what's happening inside our heads. I have to tell you, I got to thinking last night about what you said about wanting to be married, having kids. I did a lot of thinking about it. And I have to be straight with you and tell you I'm not into that number. I don't know what I'd like for us, but I'd like it to be you and me. I can't project, Sidonie. That's my hangup. The minute I start projecting and get the mental rushes on a lot of domestic scenes, I start getting very antsy, uptight. It looks so tied-down, so boring. I'd hate to start feeling that way about being with you. Because it's not how I feel now. Now, it's a high, a good trip. A great trip. But that married number, moving out of town and starting the baby bit, it's such a slow scene, such a drag. A whole bag of heavy responsibilities when you're not even sure if what you're into is any good. I don't know about kids. Having one crawling around the studio, getting in my way while I'm trying to work. That whole business with the zoo and horsing around. I'm never going to be one of the types who leaves at eight and comes home at six. I couldn't hack that kind of day-after-day hassle. I hate all that, babe. That's where I grew up. It's stifling, a fucking bummer. Smothers all the creativity right out of you. But maybe in town, maybe like that we could get something together.

I'm high on you. Just thinking about you's a groove."

"The only thing I'm interested in right now," she said, doing the very thing he said he couldn't: projecting, "is taking a cooking course. And that only makes me a housewife in another disguise."

"No, it doesn't."

"You don't think so?" Her eyes questioned his.

"Listen, I'm doing what *I* want. Why shouldn't you do what *you* want?"

You're playing me along, she thought, and couldn't contain the suspicion.

"Are you saying what you think I want to hear so I'll do your movie? Is that it? You tell me you love me, but I can't help feeling you've got ulterior motives."

"There's not a hellofalot I can do about how you feel," he said, pissed with her for doubting him. "It's not exactly an upper your thinking I'm pulling a snow-job so you'll fuck me on camera. That's a heavy putdown, you know. It's not what I'd call the ultimate ego trip."

"How do I know you're truthful?"

"You don't, eh?" he said with equal intensity. "You're going to have to trust me."

"Why should I? Give me one good reason why."

"Because you're in love with me and you're going to have to."

How vain! she thought.

"And," he continued, "because I'm in love with you and *I'm* going to have to trust you."

This doesn't sound right, doesn't feel right.

"It seems as if there should be something more."

"Like what?" he asked, one hand on his hip, the other out in the air like a small serving tray. "Like you want me to make solemn pledges after we've been together two weeks? Would you *buy* that? Man, *I* wouldn't. I've got all kinds of feeling for you. But what you're after, you're into taking off on a marriage trip with me, a baby trip. And I'm telling you that's not my bag but I'm willing to give this thing some time. We have to establish a little mutual trust here."

"That's the whole point," she said evenly. "I'm not sure I do trust you."

"Beautiful! And I'm not sure love'll last forever. Can we play it that way and see how it goes?" At that instant, what he wanted most was to split. Just walk out and maybe go see Grace. Who needs this shit? But he couldn't do a thing. Because without Sidonie, no movie.

"Listen," he said, giving it one last try, "a lot of chicks would be flattered as hell being asked to star in a movie. You know? And all I get from you is a lot of flak about trust and suspicion and the whole thing? I want you for the movie. I'm going to make you beautiful. You *are* beautiful. I'll make you even more. Will you just please relax and go along for the ride? You've got nothing to lose and all kinds of gains to make. Give us some time, babe."

"Time," she repeated dumbly. "It's all I've got lots of."

They didn't go out after all. Because to convince her and quiet her, they went into her bedroom.

"Every time your clothes come off, it's like Christmas," he said, his hands laying claim to her breasts, his mouth moving in on hers.

She sighed, falling back.

"The way you talk," she said, stopping his hands for a moment. "Did you always talk that way?"

"What? What way?"

"Slangy."

"I talk the way I talk. Right now, nobody's talking."

He's right, she thought, I *am* easy. Just look how easy I am! A hand between her legs or a hand on her breast and she was off, chugging like a small steam engine climbing the side of a mountain. Feeling a kind of dull despair as he began, all too easily, stimulating her. And such a willing victim, reversing their positions, gladly probed by his tongue while her hands and mouth played him like some perversely pleasure-giving but highly lethal weapon. Her breasts hanging down, swaying. Don't think! Don't look! Just close your eyes and climb on board as the slow uphill climb commences. I wish I didn't like this. I wish you had no effect on me at all, that I could just go cold and motionless and empty the way I used to with Frank. But no. You're down there attached to me like a suction pump, making me forget everything but how to move, how to dip and grind and swivel with all the vulgar grandeur of a cheap stripper.

NINE

U nable to face the prospect of another visit to Aunt Claudia with nothing tangible accomplished, she began looking for and found an exclusive school offering a Cordon Bleu certificate course and went down to have a chat with the proprietor and enroll for the next course, commencing in January.

She felt inordinately pleased with herself at having finally taken a positive step forward. If worse came to worse, with certification, she'd be able to get work somewhere in the catering field. And while the idea of finding herself all decked out in white behind the stainless steel counters and swing-doors of some restaurant hadn't any real appeal, at least she was going to be working toward the acquisition of some marketable ability. Better than frying hamburgers in some greasy spoon.

It seemed she'd scarcely had time to consider the implications involved when Michael announced, "We're going to start shooting the exteriors at the end

169

of this week." She signed the contracts he brought in a state of aroused distraction, beginning to loathe herself for being so subjective, for being every bit as easy as he'd claimed. Every time she saw him, every time she heard his voice, every time he put his hands on her, her will vanished. Her increasing capacities frightened her. He seemed to want to prove how insatiable she was, making her come again and again until she felt crippled inside and out; until she felt sick with remorse.

Despite all his assurances and long speeches about artistic integrity and her extremely photogenic qualities, she was very uneasy. Especially when he convinced her to let him take several dozen Polaroid pictures of her immediately after making love. Then held them under her nose and said, "See that! Beautiful!" She just closed her eyes and waited until he removed the photographs.

Something was wrong. She felt it in his sometime evasive answers to direct questions; something in his eyes that went traveling off into the dark, brooding regions; something about her daily diminishing liking for him. It had to do with her compulsive need to know where he was those nights he wasn't with her, and why his telephone wasn't answered on those nights.

He insisted she was in love with him. But her whispering (all the while telling herself, I'm in control. I can handle this) "I love you," at the peak of climax did not constitute, as far as she was concerned, a legitimate declaration of love. It was retractable at any time. Saying I love you was one thing. Meaning it was quite another. Every time she said it, the air around her seemed too receptive, too cavernous. She couldn't explain to herself why she had to keep on saying it, saying I love you, I love you the way victims of accidents cry Help!

On those nights on her own that she had begun, unexpectedly, to value once past the agony of wondering where he was, she'd sit trying to understand her involvement, her daily growing dependence on his body and daily decreasing fondness for herself. She was being eaten alive by her conviction that he was nurturing at least one other involvement. For her, it showed in the way he occasionally arrived at her apartment in a state of wearied distraction. On these occasions, he wanted nothing. He'd drink a lot, ignoring food; brooding. Until he began feeling either the effects of the drink or her presence. Whereupon he'd suddenly burst forth with smiles and his usual embarrassingly crude overtures and she'd climb onto his lap or unzip his trousers and avidly begin encouraging his retreat from this mood.

Shameless, prideless, she'd kneel in front of him, crazily desperate to shift his attention back toward her; toward what he liked about her—her body.

"You're so fucking oral," he'd hiss softly, his lips pulling back in a grimace as his hand not so gently held her head locked into place. And she'd perform, blanking her mind to the revulsion twisting her inside; blanking her ears to the voice inside her skull telling her, You're a sucker. You don't have to be doing this. She'd shake off that voice with the same ease with which she was now able to shed her clothes, hunger making her blind and deaf to anything but the pulsing, immediate need to be tended to.

Three weeks and she felt as if she'd been involved with this man for a lifetime. He was showing her the underside of her own belly, pushing her face into the dirt of her own desires. And she was powerless to put an end to it. Because her body would begin twitching and contracting at the mere thought of him.

So, dutifully, she arrived at his apartment at six A.M. on the first scheduled day, to be made up and outfitted in Honey's first costume. Ankle-length beige suede coat, fur lined, fur-collared. High suede boots and suede beret. Props in hand (shoulder bag, gloves and Macintosh apple) she went with Michael down to his car, on her way to Indian Hill Park where quite a few scenes were to be shot.

"I'm so nervous," she told him, examining his calm profile as he drove.

"So'm I." He was thinking about Grace, for the first time realizing she'd find all about Sidonie simply by seeing the film. And he was rattled at the prospect of her scathing comments.

"Makeup's great," he said, getting a stranglehold on Grace and shoving her off to one side. "Jeanie's good. She'll be on location for touchups."

"How are you going to manage this, acting with me and directing at the same time. I don't see how you can."

"Me neither. But I'm going to. Know your lines?"

"I think so."

"Okay. Let's run each other through."

"My teeth are chattering, I'm so scared."

"Lines."

The face was the same but the man was unrecognizable to her. An entirely different person.

They rehearsed their dialogue, including scenes they probably wouldn't get to in the first day's shooting.

"Don't worry about inflection, all that. We'll get down into our characters once we start, do a couple of run-throughs for the angles, lights, then see if we can't get a few good takes today. Just be natural, be yourself. That's all I want."

Which only made her more nervous than ever. How did I get into this?

He pulled into the parking lot and leaned over to kiss her on the forehead.

"You'll be beautiful. Either that, or I'm going to have the biggest tax write-off I ever dreamed of." He wasn't laughing.

"That's precisely the right thing to say to make me so scared I won't be able to open my mouth, let alone remember my lines."

"Relax and do it! You'll be fine."

He did have a point. It didn't seem at all difficult. Just walking along the path as he told her to do, eating the apple, looking around at the few early-risers jogging by, a mother here and there with a carriage. Babies. Cold. Michael stood by the camera and watched her make the long walk (the opening credits would roll over the first minutes of her

173

walking), thinking, She's a natural. Perfect. Jesus! I was right. I knew it.

He checked the angles, lights, then decided to go for a take. And got it first time out. She did as she was told, without apparent awareness of the camera; did the long walk.

They stopped for coffee while the crew moved the gear down to the pond.

"Was it all right?" she asked him. "I felt so strange. I thought it would be different, harder. But it wasn't. Just walking. There really was nothing to it." Talk to me, she prayed. Look at me, see me. My life is slipping out from under me and all the things I thought I knew are nothing. I know nothing.

"Keep it up. We'll shoot my scene next. Then, with any luck, get part of the first meeting done today. That'll be one hellofa day's shooting."

"Yes."

"Be cool, Sids. Everything's great."

She stood beyond camera range and watched as Michael was filmed walking from the opposite approach to the pond. It all seemed, so far, like some elaborate new part of the continuing game. Senseless.

A cold, sunny morning. The cameraman, two men handling the lights, the makeup and props women, the script assistant who paced nervously, looking important with her stopwatch and clipboard. A truck over there parked on the grass dispensing equipment like some kind of traveling supply store.

What am I doing here? Jeanie, the makeup lady has bad cigarette breath and a tight, concentrated face, her eyes look like camera lenses as she blots

and puffs and touches up my face. I don't feel like
an actress. I don't even feel like a *person*. Turning
around to notice a small cluster of women with
children watching the proceedings, a few men
stopping too, briefcases tucked under their arms
or parked down by their feet, chatting together
amicably, commenting on the goings-on disrupting
the usual morning serenity of the park. Looking at
me, whispering, "Who is she? Anybody?" loud
enough for me to hear and feel even stranger. Wanting to tell them, You can go on to work or wherever you're going because I'm nobody and this is
only crazy make-believe. We should know better
but we don't. It isn't worth staying, watching.

Michael does look good doing it, though. With
his hair cut a lot shorter, but still curling at the back
of his neck. Curly behind his ears, like a little boy's.
Eyes so blue in the sunshine. Looking like a movie
star. You really do, Michael. Nobody would believe
you capable of the things you do, the persuasion,
the manipulation. You do do that. There's a word
that I always associated with physiotherapy until
Aunt Claudia started homing in on my consciousness. But I can recognize it now. God! I'm going
to have to take off all my clothes, make love in front
of all these people you've hired to play this lunatic
game with us. Real. Not faked. Every time I try
to think of something else, my mind comes back to
that. I can't *think* of anything else. Do you feel anything about it, Michael? Or is it just more of the
same but for public consumption?

Chilled, she raised her collar, hunching down inside the coat, tucking her hands into her sleeves.

They cut. Officiously, Michael said, "That's a take. How'd it look to you, Joe?"

The cameraman said, "Looks good." With no facial expression whatsoever.

Michael laughed exultantly. "Two good takes in one morning. Beautiful! Let's get it set up for the next scene."

Michael, standing beside me talking, holding my hand while Jeanie does things to our faces and Abe the lighting man holds a light meter in front of us, nodding and mumbling to himself; then taking Michael off to one side to discuss something while I stand trying not to watch but watching anyway, drinking hot, bitter coffee from a paper cup, from the truck. Amazing, that truck. Has everything you could want or need. I'm so cold. I didn't used to get this cold. Maybe it's because I'm thinner. My bones feel cold.

Rehearsing their first scene together.

"My voice sounds wrong," she said, staring at Michael. "Everything's wrong. I'm going to make a mistake. I *know* it."

"You won't!" What the hell's with you, always so sure you're about to fuck up. Haven't you got anything in there working for you? How can anyone be so fucking beautiful and so fucking *unconvinced?* "Don't think about the crew. Think about seeing me, and how interested you are in looking at me, about how interested I am in looking at you. Come on, Sids. Smile! What'm I funny-looking or something?"

176

He hugged her, keeping his face safely distant. Mustn't damage their careful makeup.

"I feel . . . never mind. Tell me again what I'm supposed to do."

He did. And they rehearsed it, walked it through. Then shot it. Then shot it again. And again. And again. Eleven times until her mouth felt stiff from smiling, and constant repetition had reduced the dialogue to gibberish and her stomach was beginning to growl and Michael seemed like some maniacal martinet, bent on repeating and repeating until it was perfect. Which, finally, he seemed to think it was. Clapping his hands together authoritatively, saying, "Break for lunch! An hour. Then we'll set up for the walk through the zoo. C'mon, Sids. We'll sit in the truck where it's warm."

He had—out of nowhere—started calling her this silly nickname. She wondered why he thought she'd like having her name altered that way.

"That wasn't your fault, Sids," he explained, referring to the eleven takes, sitting on an equipment box in the back of the truck. "I was trying for the right tone, mood. I think we've got it down. If we don't get off with the right feel, it'll bomb, I'll be walking around town trying to distribute a turkey. But we've got it. Eleven takes isn't bad, you know. Course, we don't do anywhere near that many takes on a skin flick. We don't go for effect. Just the cunt shots, action."

"I hate hearing about that," she said quietly, looking away.

"So don't listen!" he said, looking distant.

Unrecognizable. I don't know you, Michael. Your eyes take off somewhere, your brain too. Working out God-knows-what to heighten the effects of this ludicrous venture.

"I've enrolled for a course."

"Great, Sids!"

Not even hearing me.

She sat on the cold folding chair and drank another cup of coffee, refusing the curled-at-the-edges sandwiches Jeanie offered everyone. Her stomach recoiled at the sight of them Those sandwiches from the coffee shop on the far side of the park. Lillian, the script assistant, had hiked all the way across the Park to get everyone lunch. She's always moving, always eyeing her stopwatch, her clipboard. Making little notes. Doing this and that. As if she knows what she's doing. They all look as if they know what they're doing. If only I knew what I'm supposed to be doing.

"Try for an amused expression, Sids. It's got to be plain to the audience you like him right off, you're amused by him, want him. Small smiles. Let your eyes talk."

Words. Words and directions. Stand here, sit there, say this, look that way, do this, do that. I'm becoming split inside, can feel it happening. Part of me watching *her* doing everything he wants, the other part of me deep deep in here feeling sadder, more and more depressed, confused, lost. I'm not here, Michael. I'm not where you can see me. I'm not Honey. I'm me. Inside, I'm me. My name is

Sidonie Elizabeth Graham. And I think I'm changing. Or becoming. Or maybe stopping being a little girl.

Thinking about dying. Vague, indefinite thoughts about death. Wanting my life back the way it used to be. When I was little. But it's going, dying. I can't ever be that way, not ever again. Because you're taking me, making me look, forcing me to grow in self-defense. If I don't, if I remain that little girl, you'll devour me. You'll eat me up, then spit out my bones and step over them on your way somewhere else.

"You want me to laugh right here?"

"Right. Nice, light laugh."

"Good girl."

I'm an automaton with a voice. I'll be a good girl and do everything you ask. I'll even take my clothes off and make love to you. Because *you* need this. And suddenly I can see that. It's your need, not mine. My God! I can see it now! It's as if that little girl inside me is running to catch up, gathering years like bouquets of flowers along the way; running with an armful of years To meet me here in the middle of nowhere.

When this is over, I'll start my classes and do a little more work on my apartment; condition myself to the fact that it's my place, the place where I live. No more pretending it's temporary. It may be permanent. I'm going to do the things I want to do. And I'll get over you, stop wanting you, stop hating myself for wanting you.

Seventeen days of shooting to do all the location work, including scenes that came at the end or somewhere in the middle. She found it almost impossible to keep track of where the individual scenes fit into the whole.

They moved downtown. Michael had spoken to the bank manager, promised him a credit. Thank you Bank for Michael's daily bread. We must all do our bit to make Michael's dreams come true. She watched him offer the bank guard two hundred dollars to play himself, then stood by watching him talking to the three actors playing the holdup men. In their stocking masks. Three days filming in the bank. And she was all eyes, seeing, absorbing, feeling meanings taking shape in her brain.

Then, on the final day, the first time the pistol was fired—the sound of the blank terrifying because she hadn't been expecting the noise—her eyes got very round, the room spun and she did something else she'd never done before: fainted. Felt everything rising inside and a funny humming in her ears and the next thing she knew, Jeanie was holding something strong-smelling, stinking under her nose and Michael was peering down at her anxiously saying, "We going to use it, Sids. It was *perfect*! You okay?"

She shook her head, holding her hand over her mouth and Jeanie understood, rushed her off to the ladies' room and held onto her while Sidonie vomited into the sink.

"Are you going to be all right?" Jeanie asked, rinsing the sink, filling a paper cup with water, getting Sidonie to drink it. "Sit down and put your head on your knees."

Sitting on the cold tile floor in the ladies room thinking, He doesn't even care. The back of my neck prickly, sweating. I feel so sick.

Jeanie held an icy-wet paper towel over the back of Sidonie's neck, lifting the hair away.

"I think we'd better call it a day. You're not coming down with something, are you?"

Jeanie's eyes looked very concerned.

"Feeling any better?" she asked, her hand atop Sidonie's head, holding the hair up. "Can you make it?"

Everything cold inside. "I'm fine. You go on. Tell him I'll be out in a minute."

Jeanie, looking doubtful, crumpled the paper cup and threw it and the wet towel into the bin, then went out. Sidonie continued to sit on the floor for several minutes feeling surprisingly peaceful.

Outside, Jeanie told Mike, "You push too hard, you know that? Why don't you ease off? That's a very nice, very okay chick and you're really messing with her head. I've watched you. I see it. Nobody can squeeze as much good footage out of every day as you're trying to do. You're making everybody hyper."

"Why don't you just do your gig and mind your own fucking business?" Mike said quietly. "You're getting paid."

"Not enough," she said soberly. "There isn't enough money in this world to properly pay me for working with a shit like you. And don't give me any garbage about firing me. I've got a contract, in case you'd forgotten. But I'm not going to let you scramble that girl's brains. From now on, I'm watching you. I *hate* guys like you. You think all women are shit."

Jeanie came back in with a cup of hot tea, looking upset.

"Drink this! It'll settle your stomach. I'm worried about you."

"I'm all right," Sidonie said, warming to this welcome communication. "I wasn't expecting the gun to make so much noise. That's all. It scared the hell out of me."

Jeanie smiled and gave her a reassuring pat on the back.

"Nerves," she said sympathetically. "We're all feeling it. He's pushing mighty damned hard. Can I ask you something?"

"Sure."

"Why are you doing this? I can tell you're scared. Why would you do something that scares you this much?"

"I said I would."

"Well, don't let him push you around, Sidonie. I've worked on a lot of movies and I've met a lot of production people, directors. But this guy's something else. He's either a genius or he's the biggest son of a bitch I've ever known. Either way, look out for yourself. And if you need someone to talk to, I'll be around." She patted Sidonie again and got up. "We've wrapped here. We'll be moving on to the interiors this afternoon. Personally, I think we all deserve a break. But he wants to try for a wrap on the whole flick by tonight."

Oh no! Sidonie's insides began dancing. *I can't!*

"Is she okay?" Mike asked from outside the door.

"We're coming," Jeanie answered. "You're sure you're all right?"

"I'm fine. Thank you."

"You remind me of a friend I had when I was a kid. Look just like her too. Suzanne. She was shy like you. But once we got to be friends, she was about the best friend I ever had."

"What happened to her?"

"Nothing. We just moved away. Even now I sometimes think about the good times we had. Maybe you'd like to come over one night, have dinner with me and Les."

"I'd love to do that."

"Good. Let's make a date once this is out of the way."

This man Michael waiting outside, leaning against the wall; this man who loomed over me saying, "We're going to use it," he puts his arm around me now saying, "We'll take a long lunch break. Start shooting again at three," saying all this to Jeanie who's looking at him narrow-eyed. "I want to get started on time. So you can go ahead with the crew and get everything laid on. Sids and me're going to have a long, quiet lunch. Okay, Sids?"

She didn't answer.

In the car, he said, "How come you never want to see the dailies?"

"I don't want to see them. And I don't want my name on this movie."

"What am I supposed to call you in the credits?"

"Call me anything you like. Call me nothing. I don't care. But don't put my name on this movie, Michael."

"Whatever you say." He shrugged, as if it didn't matter.

"Where are we going?" she asked, her sides feeling strained and tender from the vomiting.

"My place. I figured we could both use a break away from the crew."

"I don't want to do it."

"Do what?"

"This afternoon. I can't!"

"Sure you can. It hasn't been bad so far, has it?"

"I've felt removed, disconnected. As if someone else borrowed my face and body, doing a lot of things the me inside can't figure out."

The expression on his face sent her into silence. She closed her mouth and fingered the clasp of her handbag, over and over seeing the two of them naked in front of all those people.

"There'll be six crew total. I'll have three cameras running simultaneously so we don't have to do any retakes. We should get enough footage to give us what we need."

"I'd rather go home for a while. I really don't want any lunch."

"Okay." He nearly shrugged again but saved himself and pulled up in front of her building. "Why don't you go up and grab a little nap? I'll phone, wake you up, then come get you. And don't get all hyped. This is the end. Today we wrap for keeps. I'll see you in a coupla hours."

He kissed her. She felt nothing. She got out and went inside.

TEN

They did a dress walk-through. From the point where they entered his apartment to the point where the action began.

"We'll ad-lib the rest," Michael said lightly, getting a salty laugh from the crew. Nothing from Sidonie, who looked grimly frightened. "Smile," he said in an undertone, giving her hand a squeeze.

Three cameras. She looked at each in turn, at the men who were to operate them, feeling a rending sensation of finality, of impeding loss.

More light checks, makeup retouching, Jeanie saying, "You've got nothing to worry about. I know all the guys and they're none of them the type who'll make you feel as if they're *really* watching. They see it all as composition. They're more concerned with angles and light-play than with what you're going to be doing. Are you okay?"

"Fine," Sidonie whispered automatically.

A line rehearsal. Then the lights flooded down on them, on the set. She shifted inside her clothes, skin-

187

aware of the itchy feel of brand-new, expensive underwear, clothes that supposedly belonged to this Honey woman. She looked over to see Michael. He seemed to look as if he felt exactly the same way. As if he too were somehow shrinking inside the unfamiliar too-new clothes. It touched her, the uncomfortable way he looked. She reached for his hand, again feeling that strange motherly feeling. They pressed their cheeks together. Her heart thudding, a bittersweet fondness for this incomprehensible man with his compulsion to force everyone, including himself, to the outermost limits of his capabilities; demanding the best of himself, of everyone. "Whatever you do," he told her, "don't look at anyone but me. Forget the cameras are there. It's just you and me, just the two of us. And when we start, remember it's me and I love you, babe. This *means* to me and you've been fantastic all the way through. Let's get through this and we've done it".

She felt totally dried out, unromantic, quivery inside with nerves and apprehension. And realized, the instant all three cameras started rolling, that she didn't know what they were going to do. Ad-lib. Ad-lib what? How much?

In the final few seconds before the cameras started, Michael whispered instructions to all three camera men. "Keep the shots a nice mix. Move up and back. Get clean, interesting angles. Get the lines, good body lines. And for chrissake, no cunt shots and nothing ugly. We can't do this more than once so it's got to be a take. I figure we'll get maybe an hour out of this which we should be able to peel down to about twenty minutes of usable footage. Whatever happens, you keep those cameras going until I cut."

She delivered her lines in a whispery voice, wide-eyed, looking, Mike thought, properly and beautifully fragile. He forced her eyes to focus on his, held her eyes with everything in him thinking, If she loses visual contact and sees anything but me, this is blown. We'll never be able to do this again. She won't do it. Now if I can just get it together. Jesus, are you good! Look at you. Make knot up inside looking at you, wish to God there was no Grace. God! Why the fuck does there have to be a Grace? A chick like you, we could make all kinds of flicks.

Their first kiss melted some of the mutual ice. It was beginning to approach reality and she couldn't quite distinguish between real, nonreal, feeling herself beginning to react to him. Her heart rattling against her ribs, knowing all of this was going to be seen again and again, a permanent record anyone might see. Aunt Claudia! God! My lines. I've got a line here. What's my line? That's it. *God!* Thought I'd forgotten.

The moment he started undoing the buttons of her shirt, he knew it'd be all right. As soon as she was close enough to touch, the chemistry started working. He was really getting into it, his eyes following his fingers button after button, then pulling the tails of the shirt out of the skirt, peeling the shirt back from her shoulders, pausing to kiss her shoulder and the side of her throat, hearing her whisper, "I'm frightened," which wasn't in the script but fit anyway because they were almost into the ad-lib and whatever they said, as long as they didn't use any real names and go out of character, would come over real. Real. Standing in front of him, her shirt off now, her breasts, silk underwear. Bending his head to kiss her between the breasts, evoking a small surprised reaction from them both. Her mouth opening to whisper, "Oh!" because he was making love to her more gently, more tenderly than he ever had before.

Michael in all my life I never imagined I'd do anything remotely like this. I feel so dazed and sick-scared starting to make love to you in front of so many people all watching they'll see all of me, my breasts, between my legs, I always wondered how those girls could do it, pose in magazines, that girl in the movie you showed me that first night I thought, No. I couldn't do that. But I'm doing it. I'm here and it's happening. You're taking off my skirt now. I'm too slow with your buttons but I'm so nervous, my hands shaky and I keep forgetting about the others then I remember and lurch inside so scared don't shame me Michael. I don't know how this happened I wish I could just disappear I wish, oh Michael the slip now my stomach's full of ice there's only the bra, the pants, tights, they'll *see*. I keep forgetting what I'm supposed to do. I can't get your belt unfastened. Thank God, if it hadn't opened. Stopping, kissing me again, put your hand on my throat that way when you kiss me your mouth tastes sweet Michael I'm so nervous I feel I'm going to die touching me in front of these people this is the end, the last of the things I'll do for you because I despise myself wanting you so much I'd do this.

When he unfastened her bra, her arms rose to cover her breasts, her eyes stricken.

"Don't!" he said softly, sounding unlike himself, gently uncrossing her arms, covering her breast with his hands, putting his mouth to her breast, running his tongue over her nipple, all of him turned on to full; charged with power, awareness, electricity.

She closed her eyes, feeling so horribly degraded by the intensity of her response. Shutting her eyes to keep it real, keep out the lights the cameras the people all watching from the shadows seeing this man with his mouth to my breasts private performances made so shamefully public no one would pay money to see us doing this I wish I could die, they can all *see* me.

He felt the cold air on his buttocks and wished he'd thought to remind them to up the thermostat. Cold. Sidonie. Remember who I am, babe, that I love you, that we're going to prove something, make waves doing this. It's for a reason not just an exhibition to show everybody what we can do.

"Honey," he sighed, his hands taking away the last of her clothes while her eyes remained closed; moving her toward the bed. It's okay keep your eyes closed it's real nobody could doubt how real Jesus! you're beautiful the way your hair spills all falling I'm going to do this let me do this, love it the way you always do it's got to be the real thing.

Her eyes shot open as she felt him ease her thighs

apart, thinking I didn't know you'd do that, not that, not here Michael you didn't warn me. Oh God! I let you know me too well, let you learn what I like, how it makes me feel. Dear God I must stop thinking it's no good thinking it's all lost to me anyway and nothing's ever going to be the way I hope.

She closed her eyes once more, surrendering. And he took advantage of her quiescence, concentrating solely on her body and his perfect knowledge of her, taking all the time in the world to make this better, slower, more critically pleasurable than ever before.

It's happening, oh God, my God, listen to me, making sounds driven out of myself by your mouth harder, Michael you studied me like a textbook; read every footnote, memorized every bit of me all for this to Oh! make me let Oh! GOD!

"Baby, baby." His hands lay flat down, pressing as if holding her together, kissing her thighs as she collapsed, his other hand making lazy, sweeping circles over her breasts. Then climbing up to enfold her in her arms, kissing her, kissing her until her arms closed around him.

Starting to cry. It's a death scene, Michael. I'll never be the same never, losing myself.

"I love you, honey."

Is he calling me that or playing the part? Who am I? The most terrible thing that's ever happened to me. All the mistakes I've made, going with you the first time. Did you know the second you saw me what I was? Did you plan this that very moment?

To show the world what you can make me do.

"I love you," he mouthed the words, his mouth again moving in to cover hers, taking her off into a kiss that melted down her reason. Michael, *please* let it end. Kill me now and let me go off somewhere to die, let me go home and hide.

Her eyes glazed, past seeing, past caring, into a region she'd never known existed. A dead, empty place where her body had taken her mind and was trying to bury it. Do it, Michael. I know you have to before this can be over. And I don't mind. I really don't mind. What does it matter? I believed you. It's a joke. But I did. You want this? All right. It's all right. You've gone soft. Poor Michael. What happens inside to make this happen outside? It bothers you so much when this happens. You say it's because you care too much, overreact. But it isn't me you're thinking of, reacting to when it happens. Is it? I'll help you. You'd never recover from the shame of a failure like this. I know you like the way I do this. I used to like doing it for Frank at the beginning. Before it all went stale and moldy. You're a strange, sad, driven man. I feel sorry for you. And for me. No, Michael. If you do that, I won't be able to concentrate on doing this. But you want to, don't you? All right. It doesn't matter. I do love it. You're right about that. You've proved your point, made. me see, forced me to recognize truths about myself. You're getting hard again. I don't want it to happen this way. I don't care if it's a movie or not I want to turn around and watch your face when I put you, Oh! It's hard to breathe

the first second or two, putting you inside me then coming down on your chest, letting you taste yourself on my mouth but I taste me on your mouth. Something's happened, Michael. I went away. I died. And someone else has come to live inside of me. Someone different. I feel so different, someone else, someone new. Very calm, Michael. Very aware. Very hard. Cold and hard and unashamed, uncaring. Lifting my head, laughing. I'm going to come laughing.

What's the matter with you? You don't look the same all of a sudden. It's like tripping out seeing your face, your eyes. Don't stop loving me, babe. This isn't the way it's supposed to go.

"I love you, babe," he said.

"Yes, yes," the new woman whispered. "I know you do. Stop for just a second, so I can be underneath. I want to hold you."

They broke apart to change positions, her head turned on the pillow, whispering, "Now, now."

Riding, colliding, obsessed empty faces, enlaced fingers, mouth murmuring together, rocking, riding faster, her legs twisted over his, only her hips moving; frantically, faster, tearing her mouth away from his her head straining back, taking him all of him going away, so far away, going.

Her eyes remained closed long after it was over.

Her breasts seemed to fit so neatly, so perfectly beneath his hands; content, convinced now of the success, he cradled her in his arms, stroking, kissing her mouth, then her arm, her breast, letting it all subside. Time was the noiseless whirr of cameras, the surging of power returning to him. For a long time they lay peacefully. Then, once more. Just once more, he thought, draping her legs over his shoulders to show one last time how she was. She seemed maddened, sitting up, her fingers winding in his hair, tight hurting, pulling his face against her with all of her pressed wide open to his mouth, all of her tensed, requiring very little. The cry that came from her mouth made the hair stand up on his arms, the back of his neck. She tore herself away from him, rolling into the center of the bed, a tightly curled ball, her face hidden beneath her hair, all hidden away, hidden.

He let it run for almost a minute, staring at her in amazement, before getting stiffly to his feet. Thinking *she used me, she fucked me. This chick's just done a number on me. What the hell is this?* He turned, bewildered, to look out past the invisible walls, slashing his hand through the air. *That's it. Cut it. Print it.*

"Sids?" He sat down on the side of the bed and tentatively put his hand on her spine. "Sidonie?"

"No more, Michael." Her voice muffled.

"It's finished, Sids."

Jeanie approached, handing him a robe.

"Sidonie," she said, "here's a robe."

She uncovered her face and lay unmoving, looking first at Michael and then at Jeanie, her hand slowly reaching out to take the robe, her eyes locked to Jeanie's.

"Could you give me a ride home?" she asked Jeanie.

"Sure," Jeanie began.

"*I'll* take you home!" Michael said, leaving no room for objections.

"Will you keep in touch?" Sidonie asked her.

Jeanie nodded, then turned and stalked away.

She was too tired to argue and didn't want to create a scene in front of the crew. So she got dressed and went with him.

On the drive home, apparently oblivious to the sweeping transformation she'd undergone, he talked about the soundtrack, about how well things had gone overall, about how long it would take to produce the rough cut of the film.

"We're actually in about sixty thousand under the budget. Might use some of it to throw a big bash. I'm working on the graphics . . ." He stopped and looked at her. Her face looked hot, bright with unnatural color, her eyes fixed on the passing scenery.

"I was going to say maybe we'd go out tonight, have dinner, celebrate. But I don't know," he said, "looking at you."

"Oh *Christ!*" she exploded, tears splashing from her eyes. "I can't *stand* any more of this! Take me home and stop telling me about that stinking movie! I'm sick of hearing about it. Sick of all of it!"

"Hey, babe, you're just tired . . ."

She shook her head violently. I hate you hate you using me. A red film hung over her eyes. And inside, everything was churning, accumulating.

"You used me. You didn't care if I felt sick or

scared. You cared about nothing. Just so long as you could get every bit of it on film."

"I damned well do so care! You can't seem to understand how much I've got riding on this movie, on *you*."

"It's all you care about, what *you're* doing, what *you're* investing, what *you've* got riding."

"Without you there wouldn't be any movie. What's biting your ass? Why're you so bitchy? This isn't you, Sids."

"You don't know me."

"I know you!"

"No, no. You know one thing about me. Just one thing. I'm not important to you."

"Sure you are."

"Never mind," she said, tired of talking, tired of words, tired. But he wasn't going to just drop it. He parked the car and followed her inside, followed her right into the apartment.

"I want to be by myself, Michael."

"What d'you want?" he asked, pursuing her down the hall. "What d'you *want*? You want to get married, you want a kid? You want a kid? Is that what you want? You want one, I'll give you one." He grabbed her arm and tossed her down on the bed.

She stared at him, astonished by this caveman act.

"Go away," she said, controlling the anger, trying to. "This doesn't mean anything. This display. You can't accept what I am. I'm a woman. It's all I want or need to be. You can't satisfy what I want, what I need. What will you do, Michael? Rape me until you make me pregnant, just to shut me up? You can't shut me up that way. And I don't want anything of yours. I'm not a movie star. I'm me. But all you see is some kind of showpiece you can strip down and display for the masses, show everybody the little animal you discovered inside me. But I'm more than that. That's just one part of me. But you think it's all of me. I'm tired, Michael. Go away and let me close my eyes. I'm too tired to talk to you. It doesn't prove anything, anyway. It's what my aunt meant about hitting your head against a wall because it feels so good when you stop."

"Look," he said, staggered by this outburst, "I'm sorry, okay? I do care. If I don't show it the way you want, I'll work on it."

"There's nothing left to work on."

"What's that supposed to mean?"

"I feel like a whore, Michael. I feel scummy, filthy."

"Oh Jesus! Why the hell do you say that?"

"Because I shouldn't have done it. It was only because of you, because I'm a sucker for causes, just like my mother. Because you convinced me how much it meant to you. And because I thought I had to do whatever you wanted because I *thought* I needed you that much. I didn't stop to think about how I'd feel after the fact, I only questioned how I'd feel *during*. I feel like a slut, fucking you for a movie."

"You're a slut, a whore. What does that make me? Huh? I did it too. So what am I? What?" He was so mad he could hardly force the words out.

"I don't know *what* you are," she said quietly. "But I know I was crazy to believe you. If I kept on believing you, you'd have me doing it with dogs, horses. Jump, Sidonie! Open up, Sidonie! Smile, Sidonie!"

"Beautiful!" he shouted. "Fucking beautiful! I'd better split before . . ."

"Do whatever you want," she said, putting her head down on the pillow. She shivered and wrapped her arms around herself. "Love. You think it's some kind of license a woman gives you that lets you do a lot of rotten, demeaning things all in the name of love. Say the magic word and see the girls perform! What *are* you, really? Are you going?"

"You want me to?" he asked meaningfully, unable to believe any of this.

"I really do." She yawned, pushing the hair out of her eyes.

"I'm going," he said.

"Okay." She yawned again. A bone-cracking, body-shuddering yawn. "Goodbye."

He stared at her for a moment longer, then turned away and stormed out, slamming the door.

ELEVEN

She slept eleven hours and woke up feeling genuinely rested for the first time in what seemed like years. Six-thirty in the morning and the sun lying in skinny strips across the bed. With the peaceful feeling that the nightmare was over, glad of her pretty bedroom, her clean, fresh-smelling sheets, of her having finally fought back.

She got up and took a long shower, considering her future. The worst was done, the movie was over, finished. And as long as she didn't have to look at it, didn't have her name on it, she could ignore it—something that had never happened. And when she let her thoughts turn toward Michael, there was a flinty, stone-coldness in her chest that regarded everything either of them had done with disdain and scornful sympathy. Poor Michael, in love with the outside of someone he didn't see, didn't hear, didn't try to know. Poor Sidonie, taking what you could because nobody else was making any offers. All over now.

So she could think about it.

Almost three months, I watched him take off his clothes all times of day and night. And at the last, just closing my eyes and lying there, waiting for that first contact. Like a junkie, hating needing the fix, but begging for it. Without it, the withdrawal again; the shaking, crying, demanding in the blood. I can handle that. God, imagine believing just because you wanted to make love to me that you loved me! Well, you've taught me quite a bit, Michael Quinn. Sex isn't love. Wouldn't you think, at twenty-nine, I'd have learned that? But you had to teach me. So now I know. Now, I *know*.

All Claudia's pep-talks on self-respect. Now I need some specifics. Did you ever find yourself glued to some man, Aunt Claudia? Did that ever happen to you? You got stuck and couldn't get out because you had no alternatives, there wasn't anyone else for you to be with and it was better being with someone who at least made your body happy, better that than being alone? If I asked you straight out, would you tell me? I'm going to ask you.

Skin to skin, there's such warmth. And it's hard to break the habit of thinking if you can't have anything else, at least you've got a warm body to hold onto. But you can't reach any kind of real truth through your skin because words never seem to satisfy more than the surface. They don't satisfy the me inside. That can't be all there is. Can it? Like sinking into a place where thought doesn't exist, has no significance. Just sensation. No bottom,

this place; no sides, no boundaries. Just feeling going
deep and deeper until the only option still open
is to allow yourself to be swallowed up, contained
within the limitless limits of your body's pleasures;
lifted beyond the passivity created by your brain's
dissatisfactions and beyond, into action. Through
hands, mouth, arms, thighs, belly, vagina. Taking
from the only source available. Making a circle.
Never ending. A circle. Caught within the circle,
wishing you could stay mindless within it forever.
Because once you step beyond it, you're back to
the beginning wishing there was that one thing more,
that one little all-important extra. You're back to
praying for someone to talk to who wants to hear
what you have to say. I have to ask you, have to
know. Because if this is all there is, Claudia, it's
rotten. I need more than just what my skin can get
for me.

"Tell me what you meant. I keep forgetting to go
to the library. And I want to know. Tell me."

Claudia looked surprised and then deeply gratified,
as if some long-planted, carefully nurtured seedling
had finally shown its first shoot.

"What's happened, Sidonie?" she asked, smiling
more gently, more interestedly than Sidonie ever
remembered seeing.

"Tell me first and then we'll talk about a lot of
things. How did it happen? What is it? Why?"

Something extraordinary has happened, Claudia
thought, drawing thoughtfully on her Sobranie. I
can't seem to see the child in you, Sidonie. And

203

there's something new in you I could almost reach out and put my hand on. Sitting there looking boldly back at me with none of your usual self-deprecating apologies in your eyes.

"It happens," Claudia said, "as a direct result of a very difficult, extended labor."

"Labor? But I thought . . ." Sidonie stopped, feeling a twinge of alarm travel the length of her spine. "Oh God!" she said. "Tell me!"

"There's little enough to tell, truthfully. There weren't the facilities, there wasn't the knowledge there is now. It was a long, arduous labor. The child died."

"That's why you made such a fuss over me," Sidonie said softly, "isn't it? That's why you argued with mother and, all this time, with me. All of it. Did you pretend?" she asked in a near-whisper. "Did you make believe I was yours on loan when I came to stay over, spend weekends?"

"There was a bit of that. Elizabeth was doing such a pitiful job of work with you. I could see the mistakes, doing all your thinking, allowing you to learn nothing for yourself, directing you here and there, never giving you the opportunity to make your own discoveries, develop your own preferences. I tried to counteract some of the more ridiculous notions she was pushing into your head."

"I don't know what love is," Sidonie said carefully. "I don't know. The past six months, I've hated my life, done so many things I didn't want to be doing but didn't know how to stop because I was so afraid of being alone. I got in and couldn't get out."

"Out of what?"

"Sex. I was trapped. I didn't know what to do."

"Who are you talking about?" Claudia asked.

"The one I told you about. Remember?"

"The 'wonderful' one."

"That's right."

"And?"

"Were you ever dependent that way? Did anything like that happen to you? Is it just me or does it happen to other women too?"

"What is it you're asking me to tell you?"

"Love. Tell me about it."

"You don't need me to tell you that! You're not seeking information, Sidonie. You're after confirmation. You want me to tell you so that I'll confirm that what you had wasn't love."

"That's right. That's what I want. I can't tell you the worst of it. Not now. Not yet. But I have to talk about the rest of it, this feeling I had that if I didn't ... I couldn't help myself. I had to be with him. And hated myself for keeping on."

"You're describing every bad relationship I've ever heard about or known. Did you send him packing, Sidonie?"

"It's over. How did you meet that lovely man, that Jacob?" Sidonie asked. "Are you lovers? Will you talk truthfully to me?"

Claudia laughed. "Of course we are. We certainly don't play cricket on dry weekends. Lord above, Sidonie, you can't be *that* naive!"

"Yes, I can be. You said yourself nobody gave me any chances to find out. Well now I'm asking

205

and I want to know Is it any good? Have you the same feelings you did when you were my age?"

"It's just as good."

"Have you ever been trapped into something you hated?"

"What do you want, darling? What? Where are you trying to go with all this?"

"I want not to mind. The living alone, being alone. How do I do that? How do I make myself not mind?"

"I can't tell you that. You're going to have to sit yourself down and decide your priorities, establish what you can live with and what you can't and for the rest, simply hope like hell. But face the facts. There are too many women and not enough men. If you're lucky enough to find one of the better sort, learn to make a few compromises. It's what you need to survive. If you're not prepared to compromise, accustom yourself to living alone."

"*Have* you ever been trapped?" Sidonie backtracked. "What are you, Aunt Claudia? So many things you hint at but never say."

"Lucas," Claudia said, then waited for the reaction.

"My father?" Sidonie looked confused. "You and my *father*?"

"That's right."

"My God! Did anyone know? My mother, Uncle Julian?"

"Of course they didn't know! We weren't about to destroy two perfectly good marriages. Actually, our being together somehow enhanced what we already had. Eventually, though, it did get out of hand."

"This is incredible! What happened?"

"It was an almost purely sexual relationship, your father's and mine. These things were not done, you understand. We stood to lose everything if we were caught out. I think now that was a primary part of the attraction, that risk. But I loved him. How I loved him! He was becoming desperately unhappy with Elizabeth. After your birth she withdrew, began rejecting him. She was never a particularly demonstrative woman."

"But she loved him," Sidonie interrupted. "I know she did."

"I don't deny that. Don't you think I loved Julian? I loved him deeply, passionately. But sometimes, one needs something more. Julian was never enough for me. You understand? I needed more. Lucas loved my sister. There was never any question of our leaving our homes to be together at the expense of the others. But there was a very real need to satisfy something that began growing until we couldn't escape it. I was riddled with guilt, tormented by it. But I couldn't back away from it. We were obsessed, meeting anywhere, any time we could. We indulged each other, used each other like savages. It's a miracle we were never caught out. We never were, though.

"An end was bound to come. I could sense Elizabeth suspected something. Then, I found I was pregnant. I was wretched, not knowing whose child it was. I grieved for months, years over that child. But I was relieved, as well. I couldn't have borne living the rest of my days with that unanswered question. And, after that, Lucas and I . . . it was over. There were times I was tempted beyond all reason to start it all again, to throw myself at him, mad with wanting him. But it was over.

"Don't go off now and decide I've soiled your fond memories of your father. He was a smashing man and I loved him. Always."

"No. I'm glad you've told me. It explains a lot of things. A lot. I feel so much better."

"You're changing, Sidonie."

"Yes, I know. But I'm still not sure. I haven't really faced up to Michael yet. And I'm afraid of that, afraid I'll become dependent again and go back. There's a lot I haven't told you. But I will."

"As you like. I am expecting you Friday."

"Friday?"

"It's Christmas, Sidonie. I will be expecting you."

"Yes, all right," Sidonie answered, her mind elsewhere.

He telephoned to say, "We're running a rough cut of the film Thursday night. I want you to come."

"I don't think so."

"Listen, it's a bitch of a flick! Come on. Maybe once you see it, you'll stop all this bullshit business about feeling like a whore and the rest of it. Baby, you were sensational! See it for yourself."

"All right," she agreed reluctantly, thinking, I'll see it and come straight home. Alone.

"Okay! I'll talk to you later."

"I need to get away for a few days," Grace said.

"I can only take just so much, you know. Nightly visits from you are more than I can handle. I may expire from the shock of all this sudden attention."

"Why do you always have to be so goddamned sarcastic?"

"I don't *have* to be, darling. It helps, that's all."

"Helps what?"

"Helps me get some of my own back. Helps prevent me from succumbing to the sheer blinding bliss of all this attention. The great new love must be fading faster than usual."

"Can't you quit? D'you have to keep the knife in, keep on twisting it? Could you just cool it? Could you just ease off and let me *breathe*?"

"I don't dare relax my guard with you, Mike," she said seriously. "You'd destroy me. I'd have nothing left. It's a question of self-preservation. Why don't you go away and never come back?"

"You don't mean it."

"I'll tell you something that might make you laugh: I *do* mean it. I'm feeling a little frayed at the edges with all of it. Whenever you're around, it's like that old Jimmy Durante number. 'Did you ever get the feeling that you wanted to go? Then you suddenly had the feeling that you wanted to stay?' You're afraid of letting anyone get away, so you work like some insane juggler trying to keep all of us up there in the air. Is there only one other one, or more?"

"She, uh, isn't . . . It's fading."

Grace lay back in surprised silence. He'd never

before alluded to the remotest possibility that someone might lose interest in him.

"No snappy remarks?" he asked, sitting up to
look at her. "No knife to the guts?"

"It's not like you to make statements like that."

"Maybe it is. And maybe I never did it before
because nobody likes getting chopped in the face
with an axe every time he opens his mouth."

"You know why I'm like that," she defended
herself.

"What if I asked you not to take off just now?"

"Oh no!" She shook her head. "No! I've been
through this before too, remember?"

"Where're you going anyway?"

"I have a date in New York New Year's Eve.
And I have every intention of keeping it."

"What date? With who?"

She laughed and bit him on the ear.

"Who, Grace?"

"You're jealous! God, it's divine! You could care
less if I *died* here from one year to the next while
you're out wowing the little girls. But let me take
one step past your territorial limits and it's the Span-
ish Inquisition! *I have a date.* With whom is none
of your business. Do I ask for statistical input on
your goddamned women?"

"I don't want you to go right now."

"Why not?"

"Because I don't!"

"Bad answer." She smiled, her hand gliding up
and down his belly, teasing. "Want to try for a
better one?"

He pushed her back and climbed on top of her, holding her pinned with his hands on her shoulders, his legs over hers.

"Who?" he asked again, making her laugh. "Who?"

She kept on laughing, her shoulders moving under his hands.

"*Who?*" He lunged forward, putting an abrupt end to her laughter. She lay very still looking up at him.

"Tell me you love me," she said, contracting her muscles around him.

"Shit!"

"Tell me!"

"I love you." He looked pained.

She lifted her hand to run it over his hair, her eyes thoughtfully following the movements of her hand.

"Marry me," she whispered, her eyes returning to his. "*Marry* me!"

"Stay here and I'll marry you."

"No! When I come back from New York."

"What the fuck's in New York?"

"I have to go. Will you put an end to all of it, Mike? Will you marry me and stop running? I can't take any more. I'm getting too old for the race. My lungs aren't what they used to be. I tire more easily than I used to. All that back and forth traveling, I get winded."

"Since when would you marry me? How come, all of a sudden?"

"Because if you won't, you can't come back, Mike. This is where everything ends. I need a chance to

put my defenses in cold storage and do a little re-
laxing. I'm not a kid anymore. It takes too much out
of me. *You* take too much. I need some returns.
You've been too busy giving the returns to the one
of the moment who's more beautiful than the one
of the moment before. And me, part time. Yes or
no?"

"What's in New York?"

"An abortion clinic."

"*Jesus*! Is it mine?"

She looked at him for a long time before answering.

"No," she lied, finally. "It isn't yours."

He released his grip on her shoulders.

"I guess you'd better go after all," he said.

"That's right."

"When?"

"The twenty-ninth. I'll be back on the third."

"Okay," he said. "We'll talk about it when you
get back."

She closed her eyes and said nothing.

By Thursday, Sidonie was so nervous she was in
a state of near-collapse. She bathed, washed her
hair, prepared herself carefully for the horror to
come. All the while thinking, This is it! The all-time
acid test! Facing you and your movie both at the
same time.

She hadn't heard from him in over a week and
couldn't help wondering if it wasn't some kind of
ploy, some sort of trial-by-withholding to put her
into a state of eager receptiveness.

She'd relished, for a week, her freedom; beginning to understand more of what Claudia had been trying to pound into her. She'd caught up on her reading, resumed her yoga exercises (which she'd allowed to go by the board while actively involved with Michael), ate small, sensible meals and spoke twice on the telephone to Jeanie, who'd invited her to come to dinner on Sunday.

"Les has heard me talk about you so much, he says if you won't come, we'll bring dinner over to your place. Can you come?"

"I'd love to."

"There'll be a few other people. Friends. I think you'll like these people, Sidonie. They're *real* film types, not Michael Quinn prototypes."

"I'll be there."

She was looking forward to it. An evening out. With new people to meet.

When he arrived, Michael was wearing that same sheepish expression he'd worn when they'd first met. She noticed it but was so involved in resisting his external appeal and trying to cope with her nerves, she had no time for reasoning out the why's and what-for's behind his expression.

In the car, having ritually complimented her on how great she looked, he said, "We've got the distribution deal set up. And we're planning an opening in town the first of the year. A gas of an opening date."

He talked and talked, quickly, nonstop, as if he didn't dare leave any gaps. She might try to say something he didn't want to hear. She looked at him from moment to moment wondering what was wrong with him. He looked older and less strikingly handsome. Almost frazzled.

He'd rented a small private screening room for the occasion. Very plush. Red velvet. About fifty seats. The cameraman, the crew (except Jeanie, who'd said, "I'd rather be in traction than make that scene."), and the rest faces she didn't know. Michael separated himself from her to talk to two men and she stood near the door studying the place, wishing the movie would get started so she could see the damned thing and then go home. She was right in the middle of a book she was really enjoying.

An arm slid around her shoulders and she turned, assuming it was Michael. She found herself face to face with Beau who was smiling stupidly as he draped his arm more comfortably across her shoulders, giving her a meaningful squeeze. "Knew you'd do it, baby," he said.

"Do what?" Her voice emerged raspy, breathy.

"The flick. Mike's big-time flick." He smiled, squeezing harder, his arm sliding down around her back so that the tips of his fingers were on the side of her breast. He looked at Michael, then back at her. "I came to collect, can you dig it?"

"Collect?" She too looked over at Michael, wishing he'd come back and get rid of this creep. She eased away from him.

"My thou. Hey! Didn't he clue you?" Beau laughed a forced laugh, seeing the surprise transforming her features. "The bet, mama. The big bet!"

"What? What bet?" Her skin was shriveling, the perspiration dripping down the back of her neck. She was suddenly on fire, melting.

"Man, I hear it's a bitch! I knew you'd be dynamite!" His arm slid once more across her shoulders.

She pushed off his arm.

"What are you talking about?" she asked, heart pounding. "Just tell me in ordinary English. You all talk like cartoons."

"The bet. We had a bet, you know. I, like, got him, we bet a thousand you'd do a flick for him. Hey!" All of a sudden, the vibes were very, very bad and he wanted to split.

"You bet on me?" she asked in a frozen whisper. "The two of you had a *bet* on me?"

"Now, wait a minute," Beau stalled, knowing he'd really blown it.

"The *two* of you, you *bet* on me."

Oh God I want to die, get out of here away from these people away from you how could you? I knew. I knew. She turned, trembling, and ran for the door. Out of the corner of her eyes, she saw Michael turning. She ran faster. No time to wait for the elevator. No time. Get away. Pulling open the heavy EXIT door, running down the steel fire stairs. Flight after flight. Eleven stories. Running. A thin, animal sound emerging from her throat as she ran, heels clattering, echoing in the stairwell. Running faster, faster. Heart drumming, tears, racing down the stairs, rounding corners, down the landing to the next flight, the next, flying down. Then finding herself in the basement of the building, she'd run too

far. Pushing through another unwieldy fire door
into a vast, noisy furnace room. Running along the
aisleway between noisy, so noisy the noise terrible,
levels of machinery. Finding doors, pushing through
to find more stairs, leading up, out. To a dark
alleyway. Turning frantically, trying to find a way
out. Seeing the street down there, cars passing.

She stopped a taxi and sat huddled by the door,
money in hand, ready to alight the instant the car
stopped. Through the front door, down the hall,
stabbing the key into the lock, getting the door
open, dashing inside to lock the door, then to stand
violently trembling staring into the dark living room.
What to do? Where to go? Nowhere to go. Nothing
to do. It was all done. Done. She hurried into the
bedroom to throw her coat and bag on the floor,
remove her dress, underwear, tights. Naked, shivering, nipples puckered with the cold. Robe, I want
my robe. Pulling on the robe, belting it tight, tight; to
hold me together, keep me together. Somebody help
me. I want to die.

Mike hit him. All conversations died abruptly,
all heads turned to see Mike hit him, sending Beau
sprawling on his back on the floor, a worm of blood
crawling from his nostril. Nobody moved. Not until
Mike tore the fire extinguisher off the wall and
raised it over his head. He was going to kill Beau.
They all knew it. But still nobody moved. Until the
very last minute when Lillian, loathing both of them,
calmly stepped in front of Mike to say, "You've
made your point."

"Get him out of here!" Mike shouted, his voice thick as clotting blood, his fists still clenched. He turned and walked down the corridors toward the control room, toward the telephone in there. He had to explain, make her understand. And he didn't know why he felt he had to. Everything was going bad, going wrong, falling apart. People, these people fucking up his movie.

TWELVE

She'd fallen asleep. Just lay down to rest her head, to try to think. And she'd fallen asleep. She woke up with a terrible start when the telephone rang; her heart leaping into high-speed action. She sat breathing fast, staring at the telephone, knowing who it was. Stop ringing! Stop! She couldn't stand the ringing. But it went on and on. And finally, stopped. When it did, she sat a moment longer, her breathing loud in the sudden silence as she tried to think. He'll come here. She flew to the door to put on the chain. He'll see the lights, know I'm here. She ran through the apartment switching off the lights, all but the one in her bathroom. She lit a cigarette and sat down on her rocker in the living room, waiting, knowing he'd come, knowing it wasn't over.

She rocked, her eyes becoming accustomed to the dark, feeling the blackness, knowing she'd arrived at the bottom. It was like those dreams she used to have, dreams of falling. Never hitting bottom. Leslie

Browning once said, "I've heard if you ever hit, you know, reach bottom when you dream you're falling, it means you're dead, that you've died." Leslie, a mine of wondrous information. I've hit bottom and you don't die, Leslie. That would be too easy. No. You find yourself on the bottom and all you can do is wish you had died, were dead. But knowing you're going to have to keep on somehow, get through it; maybe go through other, worse things. That's what happens, Leslie.

I must not panic. I must sit here quietly and think.

There was a knock at the door and she jumped so violently she dropped the cigarette and scrabbled around on her hands and knees, groping for it. She found it, dropped it in the ashtray, then tiptoed swiftly out of the living room, down the hall to her bedroom, holding her hands over her ears, trying not to hear the banging at the front door, the voice saying, "Sidonie! Come on, open up! I know you're in there!"

Go away, go, go on, go away. He's not going. Standing out there in the corridor yelling at me through the door. Shut up! Go away! What can I do?

She snatched up the telephone and carried it into the bathroom, soundlessly closing the door. Then dialed and listened to the ringing at the other end. Please be home. Be there. Please. Oh God, be there! She heard the loud click of mid-interrupted ringing and Aurora's voice.

"Aurora," she whispered urgently, "you've got

to do something for me. There's this man outside, pounding on my door."

"That you, Sidney? How come you're talking so funny? I can't hardly hear you?"

"Listen!" she pleaded, raising her voice fractionally. "There's a man banging on my door. Please, tell him I've gone away. Tell him there was a family emergency. Tell him *anything*! Just, please, oh God, get him to *go away*!"

"You okay, Sidney?"

"Please, *please*! Tell him I'm *not here*!"

There was a moment of silence, then Aurora said, "Okay," and hung up. Sidonie replaced the receiver, then crept back to the hallway, listening to Michael's entreaties; crouched in the dark just beside the door. She wound her arms around her knees, pressed her forehead down on her knees and waited, hearing Auroria's footsteps approaching. Thank you, thank you. God, thank you!

The worst feeling hiding inside her own home, hearing him outside begging for a chance to explain. This man she'd thought she loved, this man who'd played her like a radio, making her give out with a music of his choosing. She never wanted to see his face again, wished she'd never seen it at all. She lifted her head to listen.

"Nobody's home," Aurora said.

"I *know* she's in there!" Michael argued.

"Now, lissen! If I tell you nobody's home, fella, nobody's home!"

"*Sidonie!*" He beat his fists on the door. "Open

up! Stop all this shit! They're waiting to see the flick!"

"Am I gonna have to call the police?" Aurora asked.

"Goddamnit! *Sidonie!*"

The pounding went right through her head, making her ears ache.

"I guess I'm gonna have to call 'em," Aurora said, turning to go.

"All *right!*" he shouted. "Okay, okay! I know you're in there but I can't spend the whole fucking night. I've got a movie waiting."

"You've got one rotten mouth, fella! You just go on now. Off you go!"

Bless you, Sidonie exhaled very slowly. Bless you, you dear lady.

"Some folks sure do take a lot of convincin'," Aurora grumbled, going along to make sure he not only left the building but left the area altogether. She stood by the main door and waited until he got into his car and drove away. Then she returned to Sidonie's apartment and tapped at the door.

"Sidney? Lissen, he's gone. You wanna open the door and tell me what's goin' on around here?"

"Are you sure he's gone?" Sidonie asked, one hand on the chain, the other on the lock.

"I waited and watched him drive off."

Sidonie unlocked the door.

"How come you're sittin' here in the dark?" Aurora wanted to know, reaching to switch on the lights.

"Don't! He might only have driven around the

Park. If he sees the lights, he'll know I'm in here."

"What's he gonna do anyhow, murder you?"

"He's already done that," Sidonie said, wrapping her arms around herself, trying to soothe the pain in her mid-section. "Now he's trying to tell me why."

Aurora looked at her skeptically. "You crackin' up or something?"

"Thank you for helping me. I didn't know what else to do."

"Oh, that's all right. Lissen, you had your supper yet? I'll tell you why I ask. See, Christmas Eve, I usually ask whatever tenants around not doing nothing to come on down have a drink, have a little smoke, what-have-you. I do up a little buffet, put some nice Christmas music on. Better'n sitting around all by your ownsome. Why'nt you put on some clothes and come on down?"

"Oh, I . . ."

"Lissen, if he's plannin' on coming back, he's not gonna come banging at *my* door now, is he?"

"No, that's true."

"So, fine! You go on get yourself dressed and come on down. Meet soma the other tenants. Eat a little something. You went'n got way too skinny now anyway."

Aurora moved to the door and paused, seeing the reluctance on Sidonie's face.

"Lissen, Sidney. Ain't one of us hasn't had some kinda bad man trouble, you know. You'll get over it. But it sure won't do you no good keeping the lights off. You can't stay hid in here forever."

"I'll come down in a little while."

"You make sure now. Else I'll come get you."

Aurora left. Sidonie relocked the door, put the chain back on, then crossed the room to look out the window. It was snowing. She stood for quite some time watching the snow fall, feeling eased by the sight of it. Then she went to the telephone.

"I just wanted to say Merry Christmas."

"Are you on your own, darling? If you're lonely, why not come over?"

"No, no. I'm going downstairs, to a party. I wanted to call, that's all."

"Have a good time, darling. I'll expect you midday tomorrow."

"Claudia?"

"What is it?"

"I'm going to be all right now."

"Yes, I know."

Sidonie hung up and went to get dressed.

It hadn't registered when Aurora said 'smoke.' And Sidonie was highly surprised to see her rolling cigarettes, passing one already-going around, taking a deep drag when her turn, then handing it to Sidonie who accepted it, thinking, What the hell, why not? and pulled the smoke as far down into her lungs as she could before passing the cigarette on to the next in turn.

She wasn't aware of slowly climbing up out of herself, up past her lingering fear of a confrontation with Michael, past her shyness at being introduced to nine other tenants from the building, past her self-consciousness and beyond, into the most completely relaxed state she'd ever known.

Smiling, eating a huge plateful of food, she chatted and laughed happily; her limbs, her body feeling freed; as if she'd been living for years and years encased in bandages she hadn't known were there and were now suddenly gone.

She sat cross-legged on the floor, listening to a conversation about how it was being small, first learning to read.

And Aurora, smiling dreamily, saying, "Me, I thought M-R and M-R-S was murr and murrs."

One of the men laughed hugely, adding, "You know what killed me? Ellbees and ozzes."

Sidonie laughed so hard she fell over and lay on the floor sobbing with laughter, repeating Ellbees and ozzes over and over, laughing and laughing.

"Tisps and tibs," somebody else contributed, sending the laughter back up the scale.

Such nice, happy people, such a great party. Her sides aching from all the laughter, she got up finally and hugged Aurora, saying, "I've had the best time. Thank you for everything. I'm going home now."

And went upstairs to fall into bed and sleep the most exquisitely deep and restful sleep.

THIRTEEN

The only immediate problem she had was how she was going to get her telephone number changed. Because of the holiday, she'd have to wait until the twenty-ninth when the telephone service offices reopened. She ignored the telephone when it rang on Christmas morning, dressed quickly in order to escape the incessant ringing.

She knew she was going to have to tell Claudia everything. Because there was no way she could explain constantly failing to answer her telephone. And Claudia was bound to be suspicious. So, arriving at her aunt's house early, she shed her coat and boots and hurried in to deliver her expected kiss and then plunge incoherently into the depths of her explanation.

"I made a movie. That's what I couldn't tell you before. I wanted to wait and tell you after I'd seen it but so many things have happened . . ."

"Slow down, darling. I can scarcely understand you."

"Michael. I told you he's in films. He *produces* them. The very first night he asked me to be in this film he wanted to make. I thought it was some sort of line, you know; something he just *said*. But it wasn't. And before I really had a chance to think about it, he'd gone ahead and started everything going. And there I was, in it!"

"What sort of film?" Claudia asked, lighting a cigarette.

"That's just it! The story itself wasn't all that bad. But he was out to prove things, make a 'mature' film."

"You've done a pornographic film!" Claudia's eyes were enormous.

"I don't know if it is or not. He said it wasn't going to be. But I don't know. I'm afraid that it is."

"What did you *do* in this film? Lord, I'm not certain you should tell me."

"Everything," Sidonie said, fumbling for a cigarette. "All there is to do."

"Oh, *Lord*! Sidonie! With how many others?"

"No others, just the two of us. Michael and me."

"But I thought you said he's a producer."

"He is but he knew I wouldn't agree any other way."

"I'm speechless. The mind positively boggles. I can't think where to begin."

"I can't think why I did it. Let me tell you the rest of it, so you'll understand why I have to have my telephone number changed."

"It's too much. What has all this to do with your telephone?"

228

"There was supposed to be a screening of the film last night. Something happened. I really honestly can't tell you about that. It's too disgusting. Anyway," she cleared her throat, "he came around banging on my door, shouting, wanting to explain. For a little while, just a little while I thought I was going to go crazy. I sat in the rocker seeing myself terrified of answering the phone, never opening the door, never going outside ever again. Just dying in there. I could see me, each time I'd go to leave the building, carefully scanning the street outside before daring to open the front door. Seeing myself acting like some kind of lunatic, expecting him to pop up everywhere I went. You know, he'd be hiding behind the front seat of my car or lurking outside here, waiting for me in the supermarket, or standing by my door every time I returned home. Crazy!

"Last night, after it happened, I went home and stood in the bathroom, looking to see what I had in the medicine cabinet. I don't possess one damned thing that could kill you. Not unless three packets of birth control pills could do the job. I don't even possess razor blades. How the hell can you kill yourself with an electric razor? Then, all of a sudden, while I was standing there, I thought, Why should I die over this? Over someone who isn't worth it? I'm not going to die for Michael Quinn. *He's* the one with all the problems. Not me. I'm not going to die.

"Well, anyway, a little after all this business, that's when I called you. Today, I feel strange. Like one of those little chicks, all wet and matted-down,

229

having pecked my way out of the shell." She laughed softly and lit her cigarette. "All of a sudden, after trying so hard to go crazy, I realized it isn't something you can plan like your coming-out party."

"I should jolly well hope not!" Claudia smiled. "There'd be a frightful number of lunatics running about on the streets. Sidonie, tell me more about this film."

"I don't know what to tell you. I did it. I felt like the lowest form of the species doing it. But right in the middle, you know, of," she grimaced apologetically, "*doing* it, something seemed to go click in my head and I was in control. Afterward, I sent him away."

"Birth by fire." Claudia shook her head. "What will you do now?"

"Nothing. Start my course next week. Try to stop thinking about him, the movie."

"What sort of course?"

"Cordon Bleu."

"How smashing!" Claudia looked as if she actually thought so.

"You like the idea of that?"

"Lord, yes! I've always longed to do one of those super cookery courses. You *are* a clever girl. You must be sure to tell me all about it."

"I will, of course. I was thinking I might eventually open a restaurant."

"Come give me a kiss!"

Sidonie kissed her, then returned to her chair, heat emanating in waves from her face and neck. Approval. Smiling, beaming approval.

"Tell me what sort of restaurant? Tell me about it!" Claudia crossed her legs and reached for a fresh cigarette.

"There's one other thing," Sidonie said slowly. "If you were my mother, I mean if my mother had been like you, what I mean is the movie's opening on the first."

"And you want me to go with you to see it," Claudia guessed.

"God! Could you stand it?"

"My darling, I wouldn't miss this for the world!"

She couldn't believe how quickly everything felt changed. All at once, she was actually going out, seeing people. And throughout her evening with Jeanie and Jeanie's husband and their friends, Sidonie marveled over the newness of her own reactions. Her mind felt cleared, so she was able to see things differently and interpret them differently and respond to the happenings around her with smiling good will, feeling she wasn't being constantly judged or evaluated, but simply accepted as she was. She drove home smiling to herself, shaking her head in wonderment. I feel different. I am different. And felt all of herself turning toward the future with growing optimism. Tomorrow I get my new telephone. And then, on the third, I begin my course. Taking steps forward.

She waited the better part of Monday for the telephone man to come and do whatever he had to do in order to change her number. It turned out he merely came and replaced the round card inset in the dial.

After he left, she telephoned both Aurora and Claudia to give them her new number, then went out to the supermarket and returned to put away her groceries, anticipating her first free feeling in the apartment. Now she could awnser the telephone.

He'd never felt so foully frustrated in his entire life. He couldn't get Sidonie on the telephone. She hadn't gone anywhere, he was positive. But do you think she'd answer the goddamned telephone? No way, baby. Goddamned women! Goddamned moron Beau! Couldn't keep his fucking mouth shut. The moron knew goddamned good and well there was no bet happening. But had to score points, one way or another. And now, will that bitch let me explain? Not a chance. I'd like to go over there and kick the goddamned door in. What the fuck *is* that, not giving me a chance to open my mouth? Getting that other broad to lie, say she'd gone away. *Women.* Fucking, goddamned women!

He hit the remote control for the tube and tuned in the news, literally twitching with the need to move, do something. It took several seconds for him to focus his attention on what the announcer was saying. But when he did, a cold needle of dread stabbed in his bowels. They were talking about La Guardia. A bomb. Scenes of bodies, blood, shattered glass, incredible wreckage. *Grace!*

He knew it was stupid, would prove nothing, but he tore over to the telephone and dialed her number.

To get no answer. He'd known he wouldn't get one. She'd gone to New York on the four-twenty just as she'd said she would. He put the phone down and went back to the set, hoping for something, anything; watching firemen, policemen, ambulance attendants carrying out bodies, carrying out the injured.

"Jesus!" he said, his hands soaking wet, his mouth dry. There had to be something, some way to find out. Something. He couldn't think of a thing. He just knew she was dead. Everything wrecked, finished. Sidonie wouldn't answer the phone, wouldn't open the door. And Grace was dead. All because he took bets on one chick, wouldn't let the other have a kid. It was my kid. Who the hell was I fooling, getting her to lie to me, say it wasn't mine? I knew the minute she said she was going to get rid of it. How could I just let her go knowing she was going to do that? Don't be dead, Grace! Jesus! Don't be dead! Who can I call? How can I find out?

He called the airline to beg some nasal-voiced bitch to tell him if Grace had checked in for the flight.

"We're not allowed to give out that information, sir."

He slammed down the telephone, then picked it up again and called long distance, hoping against obvious, impossible odds, to get someone at La Guardia who'd be able to tell him something. But he couldn't get through. He put down the phone, turned up the volume on the set and walked back and forth, his eyes fastened to the screen. After the news, regular programming began. But he kept the set on, hoping for bulletins. And, desperate, dialed Sidonie's number to hear a recorded voice telling him that that number was no longer in service. What the hell? Could she really have gone? Split? He felt scared. And the coldness was streaking through his bowels. He rushed to the bathroom.

Sidonie prepared a cheese sandwich and carried it out to the living room, switched on the set, then settled in the rocker, ready for the seven o'clock news.

Transfixed, she saw the first report, put her sandwich down and sat watching every bulletin. Sitting on the floor close to the set, her sandwich forgotten, she watched and listened, tears streaming down her face, hanging from the end of her nose, feeling sorry for everybody, the whole world. How could somebody do something like that? How could they? Innocent people, harming no one. Waiting to collect their baggage, getting killed or crippled instead. Why? Which insane group was responsible this time? When did it all stop?

The telephone rang and instinctively she closed her ears to the sound, then remembered only two people had her new number and went to answer.

"Are you watching television?" Claudia asked in a voice Sidonie scarcely recognized.

"It's the worst thing I've ever seen."

"Come stay the night, Sidonie. I'd be glad of your company. This is too much without someone to talk to."

"I'll be there in twenty minutes."

He was freaking out. He knew it. There had to be some way he could find out. Every time he thought of Grace possibly lying dead in the terminal, his intestines went into a spasm, doubling him over. He was crippled by regret. About everything. He was sorry for every wrong thing he'd ever done that he'd rationalized into rightness. That new script, and he was going to try to talk Sidonie into doing it. Forget that! He'd done it to Grace at the beginning. A different kind of number but the same, the same. Loving the idea of having her hung up over him. And when she'd run from him to someone else, he'd set out to wreck her marriage, to force her into making comparisons so damaging there was no way on earth the marriage could've survived. She would run. He'd follow. Then he'd let her sit for a week or a month until he had to go back, if only out of curiosity. And finally, she gave up trying to get away. That was when she'd begun allowing her thoughts to surface, vitriolic words and comments escaping unchecked from her mouth.

I made you that way, he thought, returning to the bathroom. I did it to you. And the others. Sidonie too. Here I was going to try to do it to Sidonie again. Leave her alone. I'd say I'm sorry now, make it up to you, to Sidonie. He stopped the flow of his thoughts for a moment to listen to the latest bulletin. No names. Sure no names. They don't want everybody flying down there. How the fuck can I find out?

I don't feel as bad about Sidonie, though. It's great, the flick. And can I help it if she feels that way? That's her problem if she's on a guilt trip. I'm sorry for that business with Beau. I'll send her a telegram. Sorry. No. Write her a letter. I'll do that, write a letter. As soon as I find out about Grace.

"They're all mad!" Claudia said soberly, for once looking every bit her age. And then some. "What *can* they hope to accomplish with their bombs?"

"I don't know. It's so senseless."

"Switch off the set, there's a good girl. I've had quite enough for one evening."

Sidonie got up and turned off the set, then stood staring out the window. "It's really coming down," she observed. "Good sticking snow. Everything gets so quiet when it snows. Ever notice that, how quiet it gets?"

She watched the snow drifting down past the windows, watched the way it seemed magnified by the streetlights—a halo of snow around every light. The prints she'd made when arriving were nothing more than shallow dents now.

"The end," Claudia said quietly, "of another year."

They sat talking soberly, Anna periodically refilled their wine glasses and, finally, bade them both goodnight.

He undressed and climbed into bed feeling as if he'd aged forty years. Positive he wouldn't sleep, he turned off the bedside light and crossed his arms behind his head, staring off into space.

Ten-thirty and in bed. Alone. With an aching gut and cold feet. My damned feet are freezing. I hate sleeping alone. Grace, are you dead? I swear to God I don't want you dead. Maybe I've thought a lot of times about wanting you gone. But not dead.

If you're dead, what the hell'll I do? Where'll I go when there's no one else I want to see? Jesus! I'd give a lot to take it all back, change things. I can't handle the idea of you lying there under all that shattered glass. With my kid in you. I need a cigarette. I don't have a cigarette, I'll go right outa my fucking skull.

He put the light back on and got up to go in search of a cigarette. And he found a box Sidonie had left on the kitchen counter. Lit one, then held the box in his hand. Benson and Hedges. Soon as I know about Grace, I'll write you a letter.

The telephone rang. He ran for it.

"Mike?"

"*Grace?*" He couldn't believe it. "Where are you? D'you get hurt? You okay?"

"I had this rare intuitive sensation you might actually give a damn, so I thought I'd call and let you know I'm all right."

"Are you? You're not hurt? Where are you?"

"I'm at my hotel. Am I deceiving myself or do you sound as if you're actually concerned about my well-being?"

"Listen, Grace, come back. Don't do anything. Just come back!"

"What do you mean, 'don't do anything?' "

"What it sounds like. Jesus, Grace!" The shaking started in his legs and worked its way rapidly upward through his body until it had hold of his throat and was choking him. "Come back," he said, huskily. "Don't do it. I know it's my kid."

Grace sat down.

"Is this *you*?" she asked. "Is this just tonight's mood or have I died and gone to heaven?"

"You want me to come down there and bring you back?"

"No. I want an explanation for this change of heart."

"I thought you were dead," he said bluntly. "Jesus, I thought you were and I was going crazy here not knowing what to do, who to call. You didn't get hurt?"

"A scratch," she said, afraid to believe in the transformation. "I'm all right."

"Come home," he pleaded. "Get the next flight out. You can get something from Kennedy. I'll be at the airport to meet you. Make a reservation right now, this minute, then call me back and let me know."

"We're talking about a baby here, Mike. Not something that'll go away by itself in a couple of weeks. There's no part-time business with a baby. It isn't something I'm in the mood to do alone."

"Just make a reservation and call me right back. Now!"

"All right. I'll call you back."

He hung up and went to the bedroom to get

dressed. His appetite was back. He pulled on his clothes, trying to estimate how long it would take him to drive to the airport and where he could get a decent meal this time of night. Jesus! He'd been so goddamned scared. Just like that bitch to scare hell out of him one way or another. Damn Grace anyway.

Grace continued to sit on the edge of the bed in her hotel room, thinking. Fingering the cut on her cheek, thinking. For fifteen years I've let him come and go at his choosing. Never any warning. Disappointments one after another. The women. How many others have you broken the way you break toothpicks when you're finished with them? Isn't it strange, Mike? I feel sorry for those girls, the women you've led up and down and around after you. You stink, Quinn. You don't want me and you don't want this baby. You're just after insurance. A warm bed to go to on cold nights. Not this time, Mike. No more. It's too late and I've already made my appointment.

What I think I'll do, I think I'll go down to the bar and have a long, cool drink. Then something to eat and, after that, a good night's sleep. And after I've finished at the clinic, I think I might stay on a few extra days, take in some shows, do a bit of shopping. Go to Saks. Walk around the Village, have lunch at the Plaza. I must see that exhibit at the Modern Art. I wonder if Anne's in town . . .

FOURTEEN

On the morning of the third, she was having her second cup of black coffee, reading the morning paper when she came upon two things. The first was a full-page ad for 'Honey,' showing Sidonie in her long suede coat, the boots and hat. She stared at the ad feeling queasy. Why hadn't she thought about the advertising, the publicity there was bound to be?

Her eyes moved over to the next page, coming to rest on a long review (Oh God!) of the film. It had premiered the night before. Taking a deep breath, she started reading.

". . . Producer Quinn . . . moved up from the ranks of . . . porno flicks . . . a too-thin story line but a ground-breaker. Some magnificently conceived, highly refreshing effects . . . we feel, however, that the success of this film lies entirely in the attributes and talents of (Why no credit, Quinn?) the fragile, ethereal creature who plays the title role. A woman who, throughout, is all woman at her subtlest, in underplayed grace and gentle-eyed, knowing innocence.

". . . splendid physical contrast between Quinn and his leading lady. Who are we to knock the obvious? Not this reviewer certainly. Quinn displays surprising depth in the role of Alan . . . a little short on insight, but a film worth seeing . . . a very valid view of the interior dynamics of a relationship."

There was more. Sidonie read it all again, staggered by the fact that all the references to the love scenes were couched in glowing terms, and astounded by the copious praise directed toward her.

She finished her lukewarm coffee and was about to leave for her first class when Claudia telephoned.

"Have you seen this morning's paper?" she asked excitedly.

"I just read it."

"We *must* see it. Tonight."

"Are you sure?" Sidonie asked doubtfully.

"Don't be absurd! This film's going to be a great success judging by that review. I'm longing to see this 'underplayed grace and knowing innocence.' Come have dinner here, then we'll go see this epic."

The class, contrary to her expectations, was predominantly male. She'd expected a large group of women. There were only four women and eleven men. And before the session got underway, a vaguely familiar-looking man who'd been giving her puzzling looks from the moment she arrived, approached her, saying, "Aren't you Sidonie?"

"I am,, yes." She knew she knew him and studied

him trying to remember. Sandy hair, receding hair-line, pleasant brown eyes, glasses, a nice unremarkable face. A tall man in slacks, shirt and sport jacket.

"You don't remember me," he said. "We went to high school together. I'm Dan Durant. Ring any bells?"

She kept looking at him, feeling recognition tugging at her memory. "Basketball? Weren't you on the basketball team?"

"Right! You remember. What a surprise, seeing you here! This is really something." He laughed. "We have to have a good, long talk about old times. What've you been doing all these years?"

"Nothing very exciting."

"I knew I knew you," he laughed again. "It's really great to see you. I used to wonder whatever had become of you."

"You did? But we didn't even know each other."

"We have to talk. How about lunch?"

"All right. Fine."

"It finally got so bad I just couldn't take any more," Dan was saying, pushing away his half-finished club sandwich. "I couldn't understand what had happened. I'd try to talk to her and her mind would be off somewhere. Not hearing. Then, she'd accuse me of never being interested in the things *she* wanted to talk about. But when she did talk, she wasn't really saying anything. Just a lot of growing hostility. And she brought all of it, every bit of her life to bed with her. As if she had this list of grievances she couldn't make a move without. She'd accuse me of not noticing her. But the times I did, she wasn't in the mood or angry with me for something. Half the time I didn't have a clue what it was I supposedly did. We'd go to a party and she'd hide in some corner, watching everybody. Then, on the way home, she'd accuse me of having deprived her of all her friends. The truth was, she'd dropped them all when we got married. I don't know. Between all that and hating my commuting into town every day, hating banking, wondering why in hell I'd ever gone into it in the first place, I just got to the end of the line. With all of it. So I left. And she got married again three months later. Anyway, I resigned from the bank and decided for once in my life I'd do some of the things I've always wanted to do and enjoy being free, having the chance to do whatever I felt like doing."

"You were married to me," Sidonie said quietly.

"How's that again?" He looked nonplussed.

"Your wife. You've described me, the way I was until last summer."

"Oh, never!" Dan said, eyebrows lifted. "You're not anything like Judy."

"But I was. I could see it when you started talking about her. It gave me the strangest feeling, as if I was suddenly getting the corresponding perspective. Maybe I wasn't exactly like her, but a lot of it sounds like me. I was the one who left, but he had to make a gesture, couldn't allow me to be the one to do the leaving. So he packed his bags and took off convinced, I'm positive, that that move would keep me in my place. Hearing you talk now, I got this other image of myself and I realize it probably wasn't all great for Frank either. He accused me of being fat and lazy, boring."

"I can't believe that," Dan said, offering her a light.

"It's true, though."

He removed his wire-frame glasses and polished them with his napkin, saying, "I remember you in school. Always in study hall cramming. I used to see you. I never had the nerve to ask you out. Stupid the things you think. I didn't want to crash the line because the word was out you were stuck-up, out of it and I didn't want to bring a lot of heavy smart-ass comments down on my head. So I never asked."

"Hardly anybody asked." She smiled. "That's probably why I married Frank. Anyway, what'll you do now that you've quit the bank?"

"Who knows? I'm just going to take the time, do a few of the things—like this course—I've always wanted to do and let whatever happens, happen. How about you?"

"If my mother's estate ever clears probate, I think I'd like to open a restaurant."

"Terrific! I've been tossing that idea around a bit myself. I guess we'd better start getting back. How about Saturday night? My sister's asked me over to dinner. Would you like to come?"

"All right. That might be fun."

She was so apprehensive she couldn't eat. Claudia

had the timetable and seemed very excited about going.

"I'm interested in seeing this Svengali," she laughed. "This potent magician who's transformed you into Everywoman on film."

"Don't do that!" Sidonie felt a little sick. "You don't know what you're going to see."

"Obviously, neither do you."

Sidonie drove Claudia's car.

"I wouldn't dream of riding in that machine," Claudia said of Sidonie's station wagon. "We'll take the Lincoln."

They parked in the lot behind the theater. Claudia waited in the foyer while Sidonie bought the tickets, then the two of them went inside. Sidonie stopped to purchase a container of buttered popcorn wondering, What am I doing, buying popcorn as if this were the Saturday matinee?

They found two seats in the last row. The theater was rapidly filling. Sitting low in her seat, while Claudia arranged herself comfortably, Sidonie watched people going up and down the aisles asking, "Are there two seats in there?" looking to this side, then that, splitting up unhappily. The woman to sit in one row, the man in another.

Sidonie munched her popcorn, scared to death. The lights went down. Claudia said, "Here we go!" and Sidonie slid even lower in her seat as the curtains opened and across a white screen, the words, "A Michael Quinn Film," appeared. Sidonie swallowed, glancing at Claudia before looking back at the screen.

The camera was panning upward through late-autumn branches, the colors crisp and beautiful, then down, picking out a figure in the distance moving slowly into range. Eating an apple. Oh God! That's *me*! She sat up slightly.

The first closeup. She nearly laughed aloud, gazing up at herself, unable to believe that that was what she looked like. It doesn't look like me. Aunt Claudia's attention was fixed on the screen. She didn't seem to be blinking.

Sidonie found herself enjoying watching. And, after the first few minutes, she became involved in the movie. As if it wasn't something she'd been any part of. And it *was* beautiful. Michael was incredibly good-looking. Somehow, even more than in real life. She watched the two of them walking through the zoo, listened to the dialogue, positively stunned at how different her feelings were now, seeing this, to what they were doing it.

Certain facial expressions, certain mannerisms and the way she spoke all surprised her. I didn't know that's the way I looked saying that. It doesn't look the way I felt.

Losing her awareness of Claudia now, she followed the film's progress, surprised to see scenes that had been shot at the beginning, out of sequence, had been inserted here and there to form a logical progression of action. Her hand reached in and she started again on the popcorn.

I look as if I know what I'm doing up there, she

thought, more surprised with each passing minute. And three-quarters of the way through the film when she saw what was coming next, she shoved the popcorn under her seat and held her hands tightly together in her lap, barely breathing.

She watched—the eeriest feeling—herself being undressed (her face was on fire and she didn't dare look around at Aunt Claudia) by Michael; saw herself naked to the waist, breasts bared, and sat rigid in her seat, her breathing shallow, thinking, Here it comes. But then something amazing happened. Three different views of the couple onscreen. The angles kept changing, the positions. The two up there were making love. No one could have doubted it. It was real. The sounds and moves real. The bodies shifting, joining, real. Michael's body over hers, then hers over his. She saw herself fall through orgasms, saw her own taut body, her onscreen face ecstatic and damp with perspiration. Michael's hands and mouth traveling over her.

She tried to tell herself it was beautiful. Watching overlapping cuts, scenes laid on top of one another so that the effect was of time passing. Not just one love scene happening once, but weeks of them, happening in time. Michael had managed through cutting, editing, to compress time, conveying that this was a series of encounters, not one. Trying to tell herself it was beautiful. But cringing inside. Feeling stripped somehow. Something meant to be kept private, personal. She didn't know how to feel, how to react to this. He hadn't made her into one of those awful women, like the one in that movie that first night. He hadn't done that. But what *had* he done? Putting me through so many agonies, and now this. Should I be ashamed? I feel so scared, shaky, not knowing how it is I feel about this. My mouth keeps quivering every time I hear my own voice, see the me up there. God! What did I do, let you do to me?

The ending had the same impact on her it had on almost everyone else in the theater. There was a unanimous gasp as the gun was fired. Everyone in the audience seemed to be holding his breath watching Honey fall slowly, slow, slower than slow motion, and a trickle of something red starting at the top left of the screen, the trickle becoming a stream, a river, turning darker, turning brown. Then lines breaking the brown, the focus sharpening, camera moving back, back, until the brown was one leaf clinging to a naked branch; one leaf slowly coming free of a tree and falling, falling as music began and end credits rolled over the screen.

Dead. That woman was dead. Something inside of her felt dead now. She wanted desperately to have her own feelings and reactions synthesized as neatly as that filmed ending. Sitting, seeing something ending in her life. Her life ending? She felt afraid, deeply, unreasonably afraid. Yet not sure why, uncertain of any specific reasons why. Just afraid. As if she'd taken something vital, integral from her deepest, most private self and without any real thought, had given it casually into the hands of someone incapable of respecting or placing an appropriate value on that something she'd given.

Applause as the lights went up. Sidonie sank back into her seat feeling exhausted, horribly confused; turning to see Claudia blowing her nose, then tucking her handkerchief into her handbag. Her features thoughtful.

Claudia glanced at Sidonie's face as she tried to collect her reactions, assemble them into some sort of cohesive sense-making entity. Feeling a small despair at Sidonie's apparent confusion. And quite a large despair at having witnessed what she could only consider a quietly beautiful assassination. Grieved by what he'd done to Sidonie, what she, in all her shattered innocence, had allowed him to do to her. I can see that you see it, she thought, again looking at Sidonie. And if my response here is one of complete truthfulness, I'll be as guilty as that man for pushing you over the edge, past the last doubtful remnants of your pride in yourself, your self-respect. Never substantial, these qualities, at the best of moments. In peril right now. Because he took you, took everything beautiful in you and turned you into a clinical diagram in a textbook. All unknowing, you allowed displays of doubtful affection to lead you into the most dangerous territory conceivable. If I tell you how I honestly, actually feel about this film and your participation in it, it'll be the last step in your destruction. It can't happen. Not now when you're so close to becoming, to finding the self in you. Now when you sit right on the very edge of your own potential. I might push and send you toppling over backward into everything dark and negative that that man laid bare for your viewing. A public viewing.

"Well," she sighed, "that's that."

"What do you think?" Sidonie asked nervously. The feeling that her aunt somehow was the one to answer finally the question of what it was she'd done. What did I *do*? That scared feeling making her fingertips buzz, making her insides go tight, knotting.

"It's a good enough film," Claudia said judiciously, cautiously. "I don't see you have anything to be ashamed of."

"You don't think so?"

"He may have made you wretchedly unhappy, Sidonie. But it's certainly not a *bad* film. And that woman," she pointed to the now-blank screen, "did a creditable job. I can't imagine, though, that you'd be anxious to do any more of that."

"No, never," Sidonie half-whispered.

"How do you feel?" Claudia asked as they walked up the aisle. Sensing how precariously Sidonie's feelings were balanced.

"I don't know. Scared. I don't know. I don't want to be recognized. I don't know."

"You haven't any reason to feel scared," Claudia said. "It's ended, done. I think, you know, you lived out a sort of fantasy."

"What do you mean?"

"I'm not quite sure I'm able to explain it. I think we've all of us had at some point or another rather fairy-tale imaginings about finding ourselves film stars. An erotic self-image we attempt to project. An effort to see ourselves. But out of perspective. You've actually done it. And quite obviously it wasn't the delightful, soul-satisfying experience one's imagination might have led one to anticipate. It's done, darling. It's not a disaster. The film's well done. Certainly nothing you need think about twice. I'd put it out of my mind now, were I you."

"You would," Sidonie said.

"I would," Claudia said firmly, unlocking the car. "You've done it. It's gone, finished. I'd relegate it to past matters and get on with things."

Sidonie went silent as Claudia started up the car. Thinking. Deciding Claudia was right. In a few months the film would be gone and no one would remember it. Or her. Her name—thank God!—wasn't on it. It was just something that had happened to her one year. I must think of it that way. That's all it is: something that happened to me. A fairy tale. That's right. Nothing to do with feeling, caring, love. No one who loved me would perform that kind of public dissection on me . . . No!

The interior tension easing, loosening. I almost threw myself away. I must never again be so convinceable, so easily persuaded. I am the only me inside. I have to protect me. Never again. I must take care of me, care about me. Thinking for a moment of those overlapping scenes. Bodies. His. Her own. Shivering. Depression sitting at the edge of her consciousness like a mastiff guarding the gates of some unlit estate. Shooing it away. Telling it, Go! Go away. Getting rid of it. Consciously, determinedly. Removing herself forcefully from something she'd done she could now see had been stupid, dangerous, self-destructive. For the sake of finding out. Being made love to. No!

As they were parting at Claudia's house, Claudia smiled and took hold of Sidonie's hand. Intent on propelling her past this time, on into her future. "You haven't told me. How was your first class?"

"Oh," Sidonie held her aunt's hand, brightening. Thinking, It's all going to work out. None of that matters. I won't let it matter. "I forgot to tell you," she said, feeling the always surprising strength in Claudia's hand. "There's a man taking the course, too. It's the funniest thing. We went to the same high school. Well. He took me to lunch and started telling me about his ex-wife, about the things that went wrong, why the marriage failed. And it sounded as if he was talking about me, about the way I was until I decided I had to leave Frank. All at once, I could see myself a bit more objectively. In several ways. And while Dan was talking, I was thinking, projecting. And I realized there's nothing I have to do if I don't want to do it.

"Like that film. You're right. The thing to do is put it out of my mind. It's my *right* to make decisions, take my life where I want to. Not let other people push me in the directions they want. It's *my* body. Mine. I got so scared, suddenly, seeing that film, what I'd done. What I allowed to be done to me. Seeing, feeling . . . it was so *dangerous*. I was a child, doing something so—risky. Not stopping to think. Going ahead because of meaningless promises." She shook her head. "I *hated* seeing that! Hated it! No! It's all right," she said quickly. "It's awful having to learn lessons that way. Getting hit over the head with a fifteen-foot-high picture of myself. In living color," she smiled sadly. "You're right! You are. I have to go home and think about all this. Think very hard."

Claudia looked at her for several seconds. Thinking, You'll be all right. You'll be fine. She smiled, gave Sidonie's hand a squeeze and let go. No need to belabor the points. She'd made them. Sidonie was at work on all of it. She'd find her way through.

"I'll see you Sunday," she said. "And be on time, won't you, darling? It drives Anna wild having to wait dinner."

Sidonie looked at her eyes, then down at their joined hands, then back at Claudia's eyes.

"I'll be here," she said. "And on time."

In a mean, murderous mood, Mike checked his coat with the girl then proceeded on inside to the bar. He ordered a drink, lit a cigarette, then turned to have a look around. And, instantly, his spirits lifted.

Jesus! He straightened. If that isn't the best-looking chick. And on her own. Is she alone? He sipped at his drink, enjoying the cigarette, waiting to see if someone was going to be joining her. Luck. She's on her own. He beckoned to the bartender, ordered a refill for himself and a drink for the girl down the bar. Then, picking up his change, he slid off his stool. She was perfect. Absolutely perfect.